Chad was holding her hand, and he was so close that Kelbie could count his long eyelashes

It was enough to give her heart palpitations, but add in his tantalizing voice, and she almost believed in happy endings.

Nope—not going to happen! So hop out of the truck and get a grip. That sounded like a good plan, until Chad pulled her into his arms. At first Kelbie thought he was simply trying to comfort her. Then he lowered his head and had his way with her mouth.

The man knew his way around a kiss. It was firm but not too hard, soft but definitely not mushy, and it was the most erotic and romantic thing she had ever, ever experienced. And she melted like a Hershey's Kiss on a hot Oklahoma sidewalk.

Chad finally pulled away. "Wow."

Dear Reader,

Top Gun Dad is a story that's near and dear to my heart. I'm proud to say we're an air force family, and when my kids were young teenagers we were stationed at Vance AFB, in Enid, Oklahoma. Although this story is fiction, there is some basis in reality. In this case it centers on our experiences as brand-new horse owners. Wow—talk about stepping into an alternative universe. I learned how to muck stalls, pick hooves and haul horses. We started the adventure with some cheap group lessons and a $1.29 hoof pick and ended up with two horses, a truck and a trailer—in other words, the whole enchilada. And now that my granddaughters are riding, my daughter is figuring out how to foot the bill. LOL!

So back to the book. I hope that I've been able to portray the friendship and camaraderie inherent in the extended military family—especially in the flying business. My hat's off to some very special and talented folks.

Enjoy,

Ann DeFee

P.S. I love hearing from my readers. You can contact me at adefee@earthlink.net or P.O. Box 97313, Tacoma, WA 98497.

P.P.S. Here's a party recipe from yesteryear.

Salsa

2 cans green chilies
1 can pitted ripe olives
6–8 scallions
3 tomatoes—medium to large

Chop all ingredients, add salt and pepper. Add 2 tbsp olive oil and garlic to taste. Marinate 24 hours. Serve with tortilla chips.

Top Gun Dad
Ann DeFee

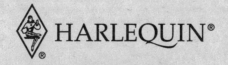

TORONTO • NEW YORK • LONDON
AMSTERDAM • PARIS • SYDNEY • HAMBURG
STOCKHOLM • ATHENS • TOKYO • MILAN • MADRID
PRAGUE • WARSAW • BUDAPEST • AUCKLAND

Recycling programs
for this product may
not exist in your area.

ISBN-13: 978-0-373-75281-2

TOP GUN DAD

www.eHarlequin.com

Printed in U.S.A.

ABOUT THE AUTHOR

Ann DeFee's debut novel, *A Texas State of Mind* (Harlequin American Romance), was a double finalist in the 2006 Romance Writers of America's prestigious RITA® Awards.

Drawing on her background as a fifth-generation Texan, Ann loves to take her readers into the sassy and sometimes wacky world of a small Southern community. As an air force wife with twenty-three moves under her belt, she's now settled in her tree house in the Pacific Northwest with her husband, their golden retriever and two very spoiled cats. When she's not writing, you can probably find her on the tennis court or in the park with her walking group.

Books by Ann DeFee

HARLEQUIN AMERICAN ROMANCE

HARLEQUIN EVERLASTING LOVE

Don't miss any of our special offers. Write to us at the following address for information on our newest releases.

Harlequin Reader Service
U.S.: 3010 Walden Ave., P.O. Box 1325, Buffalo, NY 14269
Canadian: P.O. Box 609, Fort Erie, Ont. L2A 5X3

This book is dedicated to our air force friends—
you have always been a special treasure. It doesn't
matter how much time or distance separates us,
we're able to connect as if it was only yesterday.

A special thank-you
to Colonel (retired) Jim and Sharon Faulkner
for updating me on what's happening at Vance AFB,
circa 2009.

And to my own Top Gun Dad—
my hubby, my sweetie and my best friend—
Colonel (retired) Bob DeFee.

Chapter One

"Stick a fork in me 'cause I'm *well* done," Lieutenant Colonel Chad Cassavetes muttered as he popped the canopy of his A-10 Thunderbolt. Sweat had soaked his flight suit and clogged the valve of his oxygen mask.

Summer in Afghanistan was hell. And speaking of which, the devil would feel right at home at Bagram Air Base. On a misery index of one to ten, this place was a twelve. The wind was crazy making, the heat was abominable and there was grit everywhere. Everywhere!

Then there was the desolation. Not only had the sun baked the high desert into a mountainous moonscape, the ghostly remnants of the Soviet invasion gave it the aura of Tombstone, Arizona, circa 1880.

But Chad really didn't have anything to gripe about. At least he had three hots and a cot. That was more than he could say for his grunt buddies who went weeks at a time subsisting on MREs—aka Meals Rejected by Everyone—and bunking on the rock-hard earth.

Chad's job was to provide aerial support for troops on the ground, and in a couple of months he'd be back at his home base in Spangdahlem, Germany. Deployments, temporary duty, "interesting" assignments and great adventures—it was all part of life as an air force pilot.

After the crew chief secured the plane's wheels, Chad climbed down to join his friend and wingman, Neil Spencer, on the tarmac.

"We saved those guys' bacon," Neil said. "They owe us one." The combat situation they'd just come out of had been iffy at best and really freaking dangerous at worst.

A Special Forces team had been pinned down on a ridgeline. They couldn't move without being slaughtered, so they'd called in the A-10s. Chad and Neil had come to the rescue.

Unlike their F-16 buddies, who delivered their payloads low and fast, A-10 pilots got down and dirty in helping the troops in the trenches. Their current mission was to provide up close and personal firepower for the NATO expeditionary forces.

"We were lucky," Chad admitted. To be completely truthful, their success had been the result of more than a few unorthodox tactics.

"Damn good thing the dust lifted," Neil said as he wiped some of the sweat and grime from his face.

When the Special Forces' SOS first came in, the visibility had been less than ten feet, so they'd waited and waited, not knowing what they'd find when they finally got airborne. As far as Chad was concerned, the feeling of being powerless was one of the most frustrating elements of the Afghan mission.

The war was a crapshoot, which made it frustrating. "Let's head over to the intel office and get this debriefing out of the way. Then I could use a cold drink," Chad said.

"Sounds good to me." Neil flashed his trademark grin. "I got an e-mail from a buddy at headquarters. He said there's a rumor floating around about you."

"Me?"

"Yep. You want to hear it?"

"I can't wait." Chad couldn't resist a bit of sarcasm. Political gossip wasn't his thing.

"You're gonna love it." This time Neil didn't bother to disguise his smirk. "Believe me, you're gonna be *stoked*."

Neil was a good friend, but his rumormongering sometimes got out of control. Consequently, Chad only half listened as his friend rattled on about the comings and goings at Ramstein AFB, Germany—headquarters for the United States Air Forces in Europe, USAFE.

Bagram wasn't exactly Club Med. In fact, it was closer to Club Leavenworth. The infrastructure was basic at best—the plumbing was iffy and the heating and cooling systems were primitive. To say it was austere was something of an understatement, and the intel building was no different. It was a sea of gray—ceilings, floors, walls and metal furniture.

The debriefing lasted more than an hour, and when it finally concluded, Chad and Neil retreated to the newly built recreation center. It was the epicenter of base life, primarily because it was the only place with a working air conditioner.

"What I wouldn't give for a frosty brew." Neil grabbed a handful of pretzels and stuffed one in his mouth. In deference to the host country, alcohol wasn't allowed on base.

"Amen to that," Chad agreed. He couldn't wait to get back to Germany, where the grass was green, the air was fresh and the beer was plentiful. But for now he'd make do with a cold Pepsi and be grateful for it.

"Want to hear the rumor?"

Chad chuckled. His friend was dying to tell him, and he guessed it wouldn't hurt to listen.

"Okay, spill it."

"Rumor has it that someone at this table is about to become a squadron commander, and it sure ain't me."

Well, that came out of left field. Chad was the squadron's operations officer, so he had assumed he'd eventually get the top slot. But Steve Richter hadn't been in the job all that long.

"Are you kidding?" That was the best news he'd had in ages. It was common knowledge that getting a squadron meant you were one step closer to full colonel.

"I'm serious as a heart attack."

"Hot damn! Are you absolutely positive?"

"That's what the powers that be are saying. It's supposed to be announced in a week or two."

Talk about making his day. "What happened to Richter?"

"He's heading back to Langley AFB. Apparently they have something special lined up for him. I'll bet he gets his colonel's eagles on the next promotion list."

"I'm sure you're right," Chad agreed.

Neil looked at his watch. "Hey, guy. I hate to spread the good news and run, but I gotta check my e-mail. Heather gets antsy if I don't answer her right away." He slapped Chad on the shoulder. "I just wanted to see you grin."

Chad stood to shake his friend's hand. "And you did. Man, did you ever."

He was still in a daze when he got back to his cubicle-size room. He'd wanted a squadron since his days in pilot training, and if Neil was right, Chad was going to have a lot to celebrate.

He wished there was someone special he could tell, but his love life since the divorce had been sketchy at best. It was almost impossible to meet someone on an overseas air force base. Fraternization with anyone below his own rank was verboten, and most of the female upper level officers were married.

Squadron commander—hot damn! Chad couldn't keep from grinning as he grabbed his laptop. The good thing—if there *was* a good thing—about this deployment was the communication access to folks back home. In his case that meant he could e-mail his daughters every day.

Although Chad's marriage had ended five years ago, it had produced two of the greatest kids on the planet. Rachel was a typical fifteen-year-old. Her interests ran to text messaging and her Thoroughbred mare, Ariel. Although seven-year-old Hannah knew her way around a computer, she was more interested in Patches, her equine best friend.

Chad opened his e-mail account and realized it had been several days since he'd heard from either girl. How had he lost track of time? Oh, right, he'd been up to his kneecaps in crap but that wasn't an excuse for not checking in with his kids. Chad was giving himself a mental butt kicking when he heard a knock.

"Just a sec," he yelled as he closed his e-mail account. He opened the door with a grin, assuming it was Neil. But instead it was Lt. Colonel Paul Harrison, the expeditionary force deputy commander.

"The colonel wants to see you about something important. Would you come with me?" He was normally a jovial kind of guy, but now his face was dead serious.

"Right this second?"

"Yep, we need you ASAP."

Chad assumed they wanted to tell him about the squadron commander position. But when the deputy commander didn't so much as crack a smile, Chad's radar started waving all kinds of red flags.

COLONEL KEVIN EARHARDT was one of the good guys, but the grim expression on his face said something terrible was about to happen. Please Lord, the chaplain wasn't going to show up. The only time they called in the God squad was when the news was an eleven on an apocalyptic scale of one to ten.

When Chad entered the office, the colonel walked around his desk and indicated a grouping of chairs. "Why don't you sit down?"

Chad fell into the nearest seat. His fight-or-flight reflex was pinging out of control. His kids! Something had happened to his girls. He hoped like hell his voice wouldn't crack. "What's wrong?"

The commander glanced at his executive officer before sitting down across from Chad. "We got a call from the Red Cross this morning."

Oh God! Oh God! Oh God! Chad's heart was about to beat out of his chest. The Red Cross got involved only when something disastrous had occurred.

"Let me tell you straight off," Colonel Earhardt said, "everyone's alive and well."

The exec muttered something Chad couldn't quite hear, but he didn't care. His kids were okay! He took a deep breath. So what was this all about?

"Have you heard from either of your daughters recently?"

"Not lately, and that's kind of weird. They usually send me an e-mail at least every other day. But it's been a week, maybe more."

"Like I said, they're both fine." The commander was using his most reassuring tone. "And let me remind you that anything said in this office will stay right here."

"Okay." Chad rubbed a hand over his chin. "So?"

"Your wife—"

"Ex."

Colonel Earhardt glanced at the piece of paper in his hand. "Your ex-wife, Lynn, left the girls with her parents, Peter and Florence Carter, and then she apparently disappeared."

"Disappeared?" *Who, what, where and when? And most importantly, why?* Chad was desperate for details.

"According to what Mrs. Carter told the Red Cross, Lynn is involved with a man named Leonard Schmidt, and last week she left the country with him." Colonel Earhardt checked his notes again. "Since then the Carters have had only one phone call from her. They believe she's somewhere in Central America, but they're not sure where, and they haven't been able to contact her. Mrs. Carter also said her daughter has signed all her guardianship rights over to you."

"Why would she do that?"

The colonel shrugged. "I don't know. What I do know is that your father-in-law was recently diagnosed with Parkinson's and the Carters don't think they can take care of the kids on a permanent basis. It looks like you're about to join the ranks of single fatherhood."

Holy crap! Chad had gone from the euphoria of Neil's announcement to utter confusion in about two point two seconds. He hadn't even known his ex-father-in-law was sick. He loved his daughters almost more than he could express, but how could he raise two kids with the nomadic life he led? Sure, he could hire a nanny, but was that the right thing to do?

Un-effin-believable.

During the custody proceedings Lynn had insisted she'd be a better full-time parent, and considering the nature of his job and the temporary duty assignments, Chad hadn't argued the point. That was why he was limited to having his kids during the summer and every other Christmas. And that all depended on his deployment schedule.

Chad was pondering that piece of ancient history when another question struck him. What had happened to the girls' horses? Hannah was as close to her pony as she was to her sister. And Rachel lived for her equestrian competitions. Swear to God, if Lynn had sold those animals he'd track her down and—let's just say it wouldn't be pretty.

Looking back, Chad knew his ex-wife's unpredictable behaviour had been coming for quite a while. During the early years of their marriage she'd seemed content, but little by little she'd changed. As time went on he never knew which Lynn he'd see over the breakfast table. Then out of the blue she'd announced she was filing for divorce and taking the girls back to her parents' home. According to her, all the moving wasn't good for the children.

Rachel and Hannah had been happy kids, as were most of the military "brats" Chad knew, so none of it had made any sense to him. To be completely honest, he thought Lynn missed the attention she'd had as a local beauty contest winner. And then there was her mother.

Several times Chad had wondered if at least part of his ex-wife's instability was a late rebellion against her mom's overdeveloped sense of propriety. Florence Carter was the biggest snob he'd ever met, and the old saying about the apple not falling far from the tree was unfortunately true in Lynn's case.

"If you want my advice, I think you'd better get back to Virginia and figure out what you're going to do. Word is the Carters are panicked. So take as much leave as you need. If there's anything we can do, don't hesitate to ask."

"Yes, sir. I'll call the girls as soon as I'm sure they'll be awake. Then I'm on the next plane out of here."

Chad didn't know what to say to his daughters, or what he should do, but he was the adult in this fiasco, so it was up to him to fix it. But first he had to talk to his kids.

"DADDY!" Hannah squealed. She'd somehow managed to grab the phone from her sister. "Mom's gone and I over-heard Grammy and Pops say she isn't coming back. Is that right? She can't do that, can she?"

That was a valid question and one Chad couldn't answer. What kind of worm *had* gotten into Lynn's brain?

"She *is* coming back, isn't she?" Chad could tell that Hannah was on the verge of tears, and there wasn't a darn thing he could do.

"Don't worry, punkin. I'll be there before you know it. Is Rachel still handy?" he asked, trying to distract his youngest daughter. "May I speak to her?"

There was a sniffle and a hiccup before Hannah answered. "Yeah, she's in the other room. Rachel!" Hannah didn't bother to hold the receiver away from her mouth before she shouted. "Dad wants to talk to you."

Chad rubbed the bridge of his nose. He really didn't want to bad-mouth the girls' mom, even though she richly deserved it.

"Dad," Rachel wailed. "What are we gonna do? Pops said Mom ran off with a snake-oil salesman," she added. "What does that mean?"

"It means someone who isn't quite honest." Chad didn't know how to explain the sway a charismatic character could have over someone as vulnerable as Lynn apparently was. "Listen, honey, I'm coming home. Will you take care of your sister until I get there?"

Rachel paused before answering. "Sure, I can do that. Do you want to talk to Grammy?"

He didn't really, but he was fresh out of options. "Sure, put her on. I love you, kiddo."

"I love you, too," Rachel sniffed.

That's all it took for Chad to realize what he had to do. It wasn't going to be painless, but good things rarely came with a small price tag.

Chapter Two

"That's an interesting selection of music."

As usual, Kelbie Montgomery's friend and colleague, Sherry Chambers, was spot-on—although deafening would also be appropriate. Kelbie was tempted to put her hands over her ears as Trace Adkins's "Honky Tonk Badonkadonk" ricocheted around the barn rafters.

Suddenly there was blessed silence.

Sherry shook her head. "I grew up on Nirvana and Pearl Jam, and if I think it's loud, it's enough to wake the dead."

Amen to that. Kelbie resisted the urge to whack herself on the side of the head to restore her impaired hearing. "I am surprised how well the speakers worked." This was the first time her daughter Samantha's drill team had used her barn for their practice.

Samantha was a member of the elite Oklahoma All-Girl Equestrian Drill Team. The twenty members came from across the state to perfect an intricate choreography of horsemanship displaying the best in Western riding. When you added the colorful flags and costumes it was enough to bring tears to your eyes—if the loud music didn't do that first.

The teens gathered in the middle of the arena for a talk with their coach, providing a break from the din.

"What's up?" Kelbie asked. Sherry had worked with her at the Chamber of Commerce for almost five years and they'd been friends since the third grade, so she could always tell when something was going on. No telling what Sherry the drama queen had cooked up this time.

"Well, here it is." Her friend's ear-to-ear grin was not a good sign. "I fixed you up with Troy Fowler. He's a professional rodeo champion in steer wrestling." If possible, Sherry's grin got even bigger.

"You fixed me up?"

"Yeah, I set up a blind date for you. That cowboy is quite a catch." Sherry chuckled. "He has a big ranch south of Oklahoma City."

Could she possibly have missed the sarcasm in Kelbie's question? "I'm sorry you went to all that trouble, but you know I'm not interested in dating. I have enough on my plate with this barn and my job at Chamber. Not to mention Samantha." Kelbie gave a wry smile. "Keeping up with a fifteen-year-old is a full-time job."

Sherry put on her "please, please, please" face. Darn that girl's hide. It was the same look she'd used to convince Kelbie to toilet paper the middle school principal's house back when they were thirteen. Were they ever busted for that one!

"Listen," Sherry cajoled, "your social life is nonexistent. Heck, you haven't had a date in forever. It's not normal to go years without any nookie. I'm worried about you."

"My nookie is none of your business, and for your information I took a date to the Lions Club Christmas dance." Even Kelbie had to admit that was a weak comeback.

"And you called me to come pick you up."

There was that. Who would have thought a mild-mannered dentist would turn into a lech?

"Seriously, Kelbie, you need to start dating. You can't live like a nun for the rest of your life. It just isn't natural."

It might not be natural, but it was safe. Kelbie had been a freshman at Oklahoma University when she met Jason Montgomery. The moment she laid eyes on Mr. Tall, Dark and Handsome she knew she'd marry him. Less than three months later they were engaged, and that summer they had the wedding Kelbie had always imagined. And then Samantha was born. It took another few years for Kelbie to finally finish her degree.

Flying was in Jason's blood, and after graduation he realized his ambition by becoming an air force pilot. Kelbie loved the camaraderie and sense of extended family they found in the military. Every move was an adventure, and life was good.

And then her dreams of a happily ever after, went up in smoke. It was a beautiful, sunny day six years ago when Jason's KC-135 aerial refueling tanker crashed, leaving her a widow and Samantha an orphan. The resulting fireball consumed everything. She didn't even have a body to bury.

And that was why Kelbie didn't plan to date. She'd loved Jason with all her heart, and wasn't willing to risk it with anyone else, no matter how many men her friend set her up with.

Following the crash her air force family had rallied around, but Kelbie knew that moving home was the best thing to do. So she'd used Jason's insurance money to buy the barn from her parents.

"I'm sorry, but you're going to cancel that date." She had another thought. "Why are you so interested in me going out with him?"

Sherry had the grace to look sheepish. "Troy has this mare I want, and he's blackmailed me into twisting your arm."

"So you were willing to pimp me out for a *horse?*" Kelbie pretended to be miffed, knowing her friend would do no such thing.

"Not exactly." Sherry didn't bother to hide her eye roll. "I really do want that mare. She'll make a great barrel racer."

Kelbie understood her friend's desire to find the perfect horse. Considering she owned four herself, she'd learned a lot about horse trading.

"And Jason's been gone six years." It was just like Sherry not to drop the subject. "Sooner or later you'll meet someone. And swear to goodness, I'm gonna laugh my butt off when you have to eat your words."

"That's not going to happen. Do you want to know why?" Kelbie pointed to Samantha, who had jumped off her palomino quarter horse and was strolling in their direction. "She's why. Right now all I'm concerned about is making sure Samantha's happy and our home is stable. And I'm not about to mess that up by inviting a man into our lives."

Kelbie patted Sherry on the back. "Don't worry about me. I promise that when Sam goes to college I'll worry about my social life. Here's hoping that all my parts will still be in working order by then." She had to laugh. The look on her friend's face was priceless.

Sherry threw her hands up in surrender. "I give."

Although she said the right words, her sly grin told another story. Sherry was halfway to the door before she lobbed her parting shot.

"Rumor has it the new T-38 squadron commander is single."

"You're incorrigible," Kelbie yelled, resisting the urge to give an affectionate one-fingered salute.

Sherry didn't understand. Happily married for many years, she wanted everyone else to know the same marital bliss.

Once upon a time Kelbie had felt the same way. When Jason was alive it didn't matter where they lived as long as they had each other. But that was all in the past. Now Kelbie's security blanket was her home, her barn and her town. Her roots ran deep, and that's the way it was going to stay.

Chapter Three

Three months after being called into the colonel's office, Chad had used every friend and every contact he'd made throughout his military career to pull off a major change. It was goodbye to the excitement of being in USAFE, the operational aircraft center for three continents, and hello to the more stay-at-home life of the Air Education and Training Command undergraduate pilot training program.

It hadn't been easy, but Rachel and Hannah were more important than any assignment, airplane or profession. And when Chad really thought about it he realized that taking snot-nosed neophytes and turning them into experienced pilots was going to be quite a high.

That was step one. Step two was to verify the guardianship situation. For that purpose Chad hired a private detective, who'd tracked Lynn to Central America. At that point she'd apparently walked into the jungle and disappeared, along with some other deluded folks.

That brought up another question. Could Chad really trust that she'd filed the proper guardianship papers? The woman had obviously had a breakdown, so a trip to the courthouse was the next item on his agenda. When it came to the custody of his daughters he wasn't willing to take any chances. Fortunately, all the *t*'s were crossed and the *i*'s dotted. Lynn had been thorough, and for that he was truly grateful.

That was the easy part of his plan. Convincing a certain teenage member of his family to move to Oklahoma wasn't quite as simple. Florence, Peter and Hannah were amenable to his proposal. Rachel was another story.

Even under normal circumstances teens weren't exactly known for their flexibility. Add in abandonment and a cross-country move, and a powder-keg explosion was the natural result. It was touch and go for a while, but after some cajoling, a little logic and, yes, a few bribes, he was able to get her on board.

And last, but certainly not least, was the physical act of moving two households, one from Europe and another from Virginia, complete with a couple of kids and their accompanying equine friends.

Chad had returned to Germany just long enough to give up the lease on his Bavarian-style apartment—complete with a cuckoo clock and a geranium-filled window box—and sell his beloved Porsche. That one hurt, especially considering he replaced that monument to German engineering with a king cab pickup and a horse trailer.

A few well-meaning friends had suggested selling the horses. Were they nuts? His children had already lost their mother, their home, their school and their friends. He wasn't about to pull that last rug out from under them.

So to continue this tale of adventure, Chad retrieved the girls' possessions from storage and off they went to mid-America. He had assumed the horses would be his biggest problem. Poor delusional man that he was, he didn't realize his daughters would be far more formidable.

"Daddy," Hannah whined. "How much longer? I have to pee."

His seven-year-old had visited almost every restroom from Virginia to Tulsa, so he could only assume she either needed to see a doctor or was bored out of her mind and trying to drive him nuts. His money was on the latter.

Rachel hadn't exactly been a chatty Kathy, and when she did speak, she was generally sarcastic. It was probably a blessing that she'd spent most of her time plugged into her iPod. He just hoped this was a teenage phase. If it was a long-term condition, please commit him now and save everyone the hassle later.

"Hannah, sweetie." Chad glanced in the rearview mirror. "Have you seen a convenience store, a gas station or anything that vaguely resembles civilization in the past thirty minutes?"

There was nothing but prairie, scrub brush, barbed-wire fencing and the occasional cow as far as the eye could see. Since they'd left the rolling hills of eastern Oklahoma, the landscape had flattened, the vegetation had thinned and Chad's hopes had plummeted.

He reminded himself that the situation wasn't all bad news. In the good news column, he'd managed to snag a plum job. On the bad news end of the spectrum, he hadn't realized how…desolate it was in this part of the Great Plains.

"No, but I have to go."

"Okay." Chad summoned his patience. "I'll pull over and you can go beside the truck."

"Dad, that's disgusting," Rachel said.

He glanced at his eldest daughter. For the first time in hours, maybe even days, she didn't have headphones stuck in her ears. The kid's timing was incredible.

"It's either that or a plastic cup."

"Eww!" The teen recoiled in disgust.

Chad pulled onto the shoulder, making sure the trailer tires didn't leave the asphalt. The last thing he needed was to get stuck in the middle of nowhere.

"What'll it be, Hannah? You either go now or wait until we get to Wheatland."

"How far is that?" she whined.

The child was on the verge of tears, but there wasn't much else he could do.

"We're about forty miles away. Can you hold it?"

Hannah unbuckled her belt. "No, I'll go here, but I still think it's gross."

Chad couldn't argue with that, but three days on the road with two kids and a couple of horses had tempered his "ick" factor.

With that settled he turned off the engine. "Do you need some help?"

"No!" She flounced out. The truck was so tall only the top of her head was visible. "Rach, hand me some Kleenex."

Rachel tossed her the box and gave her dad the adolescent shrug that was familiar to parents around the world.

Several minutes later, Hannah climbed back in the truck. "Let's go, I'm hungry." Although her bladder had been appeased her mood hadn't improved.

At the start of the trip Chad had promised himself that nothing the girls said or did would get under his skin. After thirteen hundred miles, that promise was being sorely tested.

He turned the key to get them back on their way. Instead of a purring engine there was nothing but a click. He tried again. Same result.

No problem, he'd call AAA. He'd bought AAA Plus to cover the trailer, so everything was copacetic. At least that's what he thought before he discovered there wasn't any cell service. No service! Where were they? Mars?

What was he supposed to do now? They were miles from civilization. Chad popped the hood and jumped out, praying it was a loose wire or something he could easily fix. Damn it all, he'd spent a fortune on a new truck so this wouldn't happen.

Hannah and Rachel took the opportunity to hop out, too. Rachel strolled back to the horses while Hannah trailed her dad to the front of the truck.

"Daddy, why didn't it start?"

Chad glanced at the little cherub, who had inherited her blond curls from her mother.

"I don't know, punkin. I'm going to see what I can do." Not that he was all that optimistic. Joe Mechanic he wasn't.

The engine looked as pristine as it had at the dealership. In fact, everything seemed A-okay. Wasn't that freakin' fantastic? Why couldn't there have been an Attach Me Here sign?

Chad was at the end of his rope. It had been a very long, very hard three months. He considered beating his head on the pickup grill but quickly abandoned that idea.

All he could do was wait and see. Hopefully someone would come along, but considering the sparse traffic there was no telling when that might be. He wiped his face with the hem of his shirt. It was fall—at least that's what the calendar said—but the sun was beating down as if it was midsummer, and the wind was howling. If he hadn't known better, he would've sworn he was back in Afghanistan.

He was about to close the hood when a vehicle approached and then slowed to a stop. The truck was the size of a McMansion, but the woman who hopped out of it was no bigger than a minute. Her size was the first thing Chad noticed, but that was quickly followed by an appreciative look at her tanned legs. With her short denim skirt, toned arms, pink cowboy boots and riot of red curls escaping from a ponytail, she was the best-looking welcoming committee he could've wished for.

Chapter Four

Kelbie was having a hideous day. Dealing with the Oklahoma High School Rodeo Association board of directors was always a trying experience. And if Sam's drill team hadn't been a part of the rodeo association, Kelbie wouldn't have bothered with the officious twits. But since they were, and she was one of the managing parents, she didn't have a choice. For her efforts she'd acquired the mother of all headaches.

She was digging in her purse for an aspirin when she noticed a pickup and a horse trailer with Virginia plates sitting on the side of the road. The hood was up in the international signal for a breakdown. Kelbie wished like hell she could just keep going, but cell service out here was nonexistent and her sense of cowboy hospitality was alive, darn it.

She hopped from her truck and noticed a tall, sandy-haired man with the build of an athlete leaning against the fender of his vehicle. Oops, was this a good idea? What if it was some kind of trap? Strange things happened on deserted highways—kidnappings, folks disappearing off the face of the earth. The Sci-Fi channel claimed there had even been some alien abductions, and they weren't talking about immigration.

She was about to take a cautious step back when she noticed a cute little blond girl trailing behind the man. And when a teenager stuck her head out the trailer door, Kelbie's doubts floated away like fluff on a dandelion.

Now that she was a bit more relaxed she took a good look at the guy and her "oh my gosh" indicator went berserk. Although he was dressed in a chambray shirt, jeans and boots, he wasn't your standard cowboy—not that he didn't have the same cocky swagger.

"Do you need some help?" Kelbie wasn't sure what she could do, but she figured it couldn't hurt to ask.

The way he ran his fingers through his hair reminded her of a little kid, although that was the only childlike thing about him. "This darn truck won't start and I don't have any idea what's wrong." His self-deprecating laugh was enough to send her previously inactive libido into overdrive. "You're not a mechanic by any chance, are you?"

"Uh, no." Did she really look like a grease monkey? Where was her lipstick when she needed it?

The man rubbed the back of his neck. "When you get to Wheatland, would you please call the AAA for me?" He glanced back and forth between the two trucks, obviously trying to decide what to do.

Poor man, he was running low on options. Then Kelbie had a brain wave. "Why don't we hitch your trailer to my truck? Then I can take you all into town. We'll get your horses bedded down and you can concentrate on getting your truck fixed."

His smile was blinding. "That would be wonderful. Wheatland's actually where we're headed and I've already made arrangements for boarding. We're good to go if we can just get there."

There were only two boarding barns in town and Kelbie

owned one of them. Marge, her part-time manager, took care of that side of the business and she normally kept Kelbie in the loop. But things at the Chamber had been crazy lately, so there was no telling what Kelbie had missed.

"Sorry, I seem to have forgotten my manners." He stuck out his hand. "I'm Chad Cassavetes."

She reciprocated. "Kelbie Montgomery. Glad to meet you. Where are you boarding your horses?"

"I'm not sure." By that time the girls had joined them. Chad put his hand on the teen's shoulder. "This is my daughter Rachel. And this little imp is Hannah."

Kelbie was tempted to ruffle the child's hair. She was a real doll. The teenager would have been equally pretty except for her "don't bother me" expression—the same kind that Kelbie saw almost every morning on her own daughter's face.

"Rachel, do you remember the name of the barn?" Chad asked.

"Uh…"

"Prairie View," Hannah supplied.

"Really? That's my place," Kelbie stated.

"Wow." Although Chad looked taken aback, he quickly recovered. "I'm embarrassed I didn't remember the name. I have it written down. But I could swear I spoke to someone called Marge."

"Marge is my barn manager."

"That explains the lack of an accent. She has a twang and you don't."

"I've spent a lot of time outside the state," Kelbie said by way of explanation. "Since you're going to be boarding at my place I'll probably be seeing a lot of you guys." She turned to speak to Rachel. "How old are you?"

"Fifteen."

"My daughter, Sam, is fifteen, too. I'm sure you'll be

great friends. Now, let's see if we can transfer the trailer without unloading the horses. I know there's no traffic, but even so, taking them out on a highway is a really bad idea."

"How do we make this transfer?" Chad asked.

Kelbie was wondering the same thing. And then she had another brilliant idea—or maybe it was just semibrilliant.

"Can Rachel steer if you and I push?"

SHE WANTED TO PUSH a truck that weighed at least five thousand pounds. Who was she kidding? She couldn't be over five-one—max five-two—and if she weighed more than a C note, Chad would be astonished. And she wanted to push his truck?

"I guess. I don't know," he answered.

"Dad! Of course I can steer."

Chad figured he'd offended Rachel's teenage ego, but his primary concern was someone getting hurt. "Do you think that's safe?"

"Sure." Kelbie's grin wasn't quite as confident as her words.

"Okay, we can give it a try." He shrugged. "I'll unhitch the trailer."

The plan was to move his truck out of the way and re-place it with Kelbie's rig. The theory sounded okay, but Chad had serious doubts about it really working. Oh, well, in for a penny and all that rot.

"Rachel. Place your foot on the brake and put the gear-shift into Neutral. The motor's not running so it won't go anywhere," Chad said as he leaned in the cab to give his daughter a driving lesson.

"Hang on to the wheel and don't touch anything until I tell you to stop. Then tap the brake." He indicated the ap-propriate pedal. "Got it?"

"Yes, Dad," Rachel said with yet another eye roll.

"Are you ready?" he asked his new partner. With her red hair, slight stature and can-do attitude it was almost like having Reba McIntyre for his guardian angel.

"As I'll ever be," Kelbie answered. Nope, that didn't sound very positive.

"Rachel, are you ready?"

"Ready."

"Let's do it." Chad positioned himself behind the trailer hitch, leaving Kelbie the left fender. "Let's do it on three. One. Two. Three."

Huffing and puffing like the big bad wolf trying to blow down the little pigs' houses, they managed to push the pickup out of the way. Chad gave due credit to the terrain, which was as flat as a proverbial pancake.

Soon the trailer was hitched, the kids were in the backseat and Chad was sweating like a pig. He pointed the air conditioner vent at his face.

"So you own a barn." He was normally skilled at chitchat, so why did he sound like a pimple-faced high school kid on a first date? It had to be exhaustion, both mental and physical.

She gave him a look he didn't quite understand. "I mostly do that on the side. In my day job I'm the director of the Chamber of Commerce." She didn't wait for him to comment. "I didn't ask, but why are you going to Wheatland?"

"I'm the new T-38 squadron commander at Perry." Chad was referring to the pilot training base on the outskirts of town.

"Really?"

"Yep." He couldn't hide his grin. It had taken negotiation at levels higher than his pay grade to pull that one off. The T-38 Talon was the air force's supersonic trainer and the last stop on a young pilot's voyage to flying the world's fastest and sexiest aircraft. As the T-38 squadron commander he'd be responsible for forty-odd administrative personnel, instructors and student pilots. Any way you cut it, this was a sweet position.

"I'll likely see you there, then. In my role as Chamber director I attend a lot of social events at the base. That's all part of the Chamber's PR function. And since Perry is such a good neighbor and a vital part of our economy, it's our way of expressing appreciation."

Kelbie was saying all the right things, but something struck Chad as a bit off-kilter. Was it his imagination or had her friendliness cooled with his mention of the military? Or could it be that babbling was her normal method of communication?

THIS WAS KELBIE'S WORST nightmare. Not only would she to have to deal with Chad on a professional basis, she'd probably see him around the barn a lot.

What was so bad about hanging out with a handsome man? That was easy: his demeanor, his looks, his take-charge attitude, even his sexy grin. Everything about him was the spitting image of Jason, and that could only be a painful reminder of all she'd lost.

Chapter Five

"What kind of riding do the kids at your barn do? I'm into Pony Club and hunter jumpers. Do you have anyone that teaches jumping?" Hannah asked eagerly. "I was starting to do eighteen-inch jumps before we left Virginia."

Kelbie couldn't remember all the child's questions, much less answer them. She decided to tackle one comment at a time. "I'm afraid we don't have Pony Club," she said, glancing at Hannah in the rearview mirror.

"Oh, no!" the girl exclaimed. "Did you hear that, Dad? They don't have Pony Club."

The club was a youth organization that taught classic English riding, but also emphasized horse care and management. The skill and ages of the members ranged from little kids with their first ponies to college students hoping to find a job in the equestrian industry.

Chad leaned over the seat to pat his daughter's knee. "I heard, punkin. Don't worry, we'll figure something out."

"Kelbie, I hate to put you on the spot, but what would you suggest?" Although his question sounded casual, the look in his eye was anything but. "Is there a Pony Club in Oklahoma City?"

"I don't think so. But we do have a hunter trainer at our

barn, so you can keep on jumping, Hannah. We also have a good 4-H club. You might like that."

Although her comments seemed to placate the youngest child, the teen wasn't buying it.

"What am *I* going to do, milk a cow?" she said with a snort.

"Rachel!" Chad admonished.

"Come on, Dad. You drag us away from all our friends and now my only options are steer wrestling and barrel racing. Like I'm ever doing either of those." Rachel's pout was sliding toward a full-on sulk.

The tension ratcheted up and Kelbie could tell an adolescent meltdown was looming. She'd weathered that storm too often not to recognize the signs.

"Rachel, don't worry. We have a lot to offer. There's an internationally known event trainer in Oklahoma City, and they also have an active dressage community down there," Kelbie said. "You might also enjoy the high school mounted drill team. That's what my daughter does. They travel around the state, putting on exhibitions." Kelbie didn't bother to explain that the girls were into Western riding.

Rachel didn't respond.

It wasn't a home run but at least Kelbie had short-circuited the teen's tears. Score one for the mom team.

Chad gave her an almost imperceptible "can you win" wave.

She noticed he wasn't wearing a wedding ring, but that didn't necessarily mean he was single—no matter what rumors Sherry had heard. And what difference did it make? Kelbie didn't care how attractive or charming he was—the man was a pilot and therefore off-limits.

When Kelbie had decided to take the Chamber job her only worry had been working with the officers at the air force base, not that she didn't like them. On the contrary, she found that aura of strength they all seemed to exude very attractive. But getting involved with a pilot again would be hazardous to her mental health.

Fortunately, that hadn't been a problem, since most of the instructors were married, and the students were way too young for her. They would've been in kindergarten when she was in college.

Chad interrupted her internal monologue. "Are we close enough to town to get a signal?" He gestured with his phone. He'd rolled up the sleeves of his chambray shirt to reveal tanned forearms sprinkled with golden hair.

It took a few seconds for Kelbie to segue from prurient thoughts to practicality. "Uh, yeah, cell service. Sure, I think so. You call AAA and I'll buzz Joe Bennett. He's our towing guy. I can give him some directions that the 1-800 rep won't understand."

"Okay."

She could tell Chad thought he'd been dropped in the middle of nowhere, and perhaps he had, but it was *her* nowhere.

"What should I say?" he asked as he punched in the number.

"Let them know your truck is thirty miles east of Wheatland on Highway 64."

While Chad spoke to the AAA representative, Kelbie retrieved her phone from her purse.

"Hey, Joe, I have a friend who's using his AAA. They should be calling you in a few minutes." She paused to listen, then continued. "His rig is a brand-new F-250 parked on the side of the road down by the Wharton ranch. It's near all those pump jacks… I don't know, let me ask." She held the phone away from her mouth. "Do you want him to take it to the dealer?"

Chad nodded.

"The dealer's good. Thanks a million," she said. "I'll see you at the Chamber meeting."

Kelbie tossed her cell back into her purse. "He'll have to wait for authorization from AAA, but when he has that he'll get out there as quickly as possible. In the meantime we'll drive the horses to the barn and get them bedded down. Then if you'd like, I'll take you to rent a car."

"You're a lifesaver. I can't tell you how much I appreciate all your help."

CHAD HAD MADE SUCH careful plans. How had things gotten so screwed up? No doubt about it, Murphy and his minions were hard at work. Chad chanced a fleeting glance at his unlikely rescuer. The petite stature and sprinkle of freckles across her nose made Kelbie Montgomery seem fragile. But the longer he talked to her the more he suspected that her red hair was a truer indicator of her personality—feisty and determined.

This move had been tough for everyone, so no matter how attractive she was, Chad couldn't afford to be distracted. His daughters deserved his full attention. And if that meant he didn't have a personal life, he'd have to accept that.

KELBIE COULD TELL THAT Chad Cassavetes held his emotions close to his chest. She wished she knew what he was thinking.

"Where do you plan to live?" What Kebie really wanted to know was if he had a wife. *Stop right there, dummy!* The man was a pilot.

"We have a house on base," he answered, bringing her back to the subject at hand. "The movers are supposed to come day after tomorrow."

"Is that right?" Kelbie wondered if he'd seen the housing at Perry. It wasn't exactly luxurious. This could be a very rude awakening. But what did she know about his expectations—or his wife's?

Chapter Six

"Here we are," Kelbie announced as she turned down the long, winding road that led to the barn. After her dad died, her mom had decided to move to Scottsdale, and Kelbie bought the family farm. Even with incredibly generous terms, her current income and the money from Jason's insurance, maintaining the facility was a financial stretch.

"This is a really nice place," Chad said.

"Thanks." Kelbie was justifiably proud of the poplar-lined drive, white fencing and pristine barn. "It's not easy to keep up but we give it our best shot. I have a couple of employees who run the barn." Kelbie lowered her voice. "But we're always looking for kids to help with the mucking. Do you think Rachel would be interested in a part-time job?"

As a mom Kelbie knew to ask the parent first. It looked as if Rachel was tuning them out with her iPod, but you could never tell what kids were processing.

"I don't know. I haven't been a single parent very long." He shrugged. "With my new job and everything else, I'm not sure how I'm even going to get them to the barn to ride. How old do you have to be to get an Oklahoma driver's license?"

"Sixteen." So there wasn't a Mrs. Cassavetes—at least not in residence. And again, what did that have to do with her? Kelbie gave herself a shake. She was acting as if she'd never met a good-looking guy before.

"I was hoping it might be fifteen. I can't wait until Rachel can take over some of the chauffeur duties."

"She can get a learner's permit at fifteen and a half, if that helps."

Chad shot Kelbie another knee-knocking grin. "It's scary to think about your kid driving, isn't it?"

Was it ever! Just the idea of Samantha behind the wheel was enough to give her gray hair. "Absolutely," Kelbie agreed as she pulled in behind the barn.

Marge, her manager, was on top of all the comings and goings, so it wasn't surprising that she was waiting at the door to greet them.

"Where did you pick up the handsome dude?" she asked in a far from subtle whisper. Chad was making his way around the front of the truck so hopefully he'd missed her comment.

"Marge, this is Chad Cassavetes. You talked to him about boarding his girls' horses with us."

The barn manager grabbed Chad's hand and shook it forcefully. "Howdy. I'm really pleased to meet you."

Chad grimaced. He obviously wasn't expecting the grip of a weight lifter. But what else would you expect from someone who was used to hefting fifty-pound bales of hay and manhandling twelve-hundred-pound horses?

"We're glad to be here, aren't we, girls?"

Their silence spoke volumes.

CHAD WAS BEGINNING TO think he'd been transported to an alternate universe. He'd grown up in the South, gone to school in Colorado and spent most of his air force career on the East Coast and in Europe. The Midwest was foreign to him, and apparently he wasn't the only one feeling out of his element. Rachel and Hannah looked shell-shocked.

"How would you girls like to check out the stalls?" Marge's suggestion was like a ray of sunshine.

Hannah quickly accepted the invitation. Although Rachel wasn't as enthusiastic, she finally plastered on a smile and joined her sister. Perhaps there was something to be said for the manners their mother and grandmother had preached.

Chad watched as his daughters disappeared down the hard-packed dirt aisle. The smells of hay, wood shavings and horse were becoming familiar.

"After we get the horses settled I can take you to get a car." Kelbie cut into his musings. "Then you can follow me to the dealer where Joe towed your truck. Rachel and Hannah can stay here while you take care of your transportation problems if they want."

"That's a great offer. I'll check with them." Chad was sure they'd be fine. He was the one who'd suffer separation anxiety.

"Daddy, come look," Hannah called out with a huge grin. "Patches is going to love it here. He even has a private turnout." In plain English that meant the stall had a small fenced area allowing the horse to go in and out at will.

Rachel was smiling as she strolled down the aisle, getting acquainted with the horses that stuck their heads out of the stalls. She looked happy—at least until another teen came on the scene.

"Samantha, I want you to meet someone." Kelbie spoke to a girl who was the polar opposite to Rachel in looks. She was tall, brunette and pretty enough to be a Miss Teen America.

Rachel was the mirror image of her mother—blond and

delicate. In a couple of years she'd be a stunner, but right now she looked more like a little girl than a sophisticated teen. Add in the starchy, prep-school demeanor that Lynn had demanded before her breakdown, and even Chad could see that Rachel was going to have a hard time fitting in here.

"Girls, this is my daughter, Sam. Sam, meet Rachel and Hannah." Kelbie put her hand on Rachel's shoulder. "Rachel will be in your grade at school."

Sam didn't say a word, so Kelbie kept the conversation going on her own. "I didn't ask, but where did you girls live before?"

Hannah spoke up. "Virginia." The child could probably feel the bad vibes that were emanating from both teens.

"Virginia, that's nice. There are a lot of trees, and green stuff there. We don't have so much, uh, green around here."

Chad had to hand it to Ms. Montgomery. Or was that Mrs. Montgomery? She wasn't wearing a ring, but considering she worked around horses that might not mean much. The way she could dish out the prattle, she'd be dynamite at a cocktail party. Neither teen had said a thing, but the "I don't like you at first sight" signals were almost palpable. Rachel in her khaki Land's End shorts and Sam in her skintight Wranglers could have come from different planets, and that wasn't good. Not at all.

Chapter Seven

The next hour felt more like a military standoff than a casual afternoon at the barn. The teens were blatantly ignoring each other, Hannah was in peacemaker mode and Kelbie looked about to snap.

"Are you ready to go rent a car?" Kelbie was probably desperate to get rid of the entire Cassavetes family, and Chad couldn't say he blamed her.

"Yeah, I really do appreciate you hauling me around."

"Not a problem. That's what we do here. You'll find that folks are friendly."

"Good, I'm looking forward to this assignment."

BY LATE AFTERNOON, the horses were in their new home, the truck was at the repair shop, Chad had rented a car and the family had temporarily moved into the base lodging facilities.

"What would you like for dinner?" he asked the girls.

"Hamburgers!" Hannah squealed.

"Hamburgers it is." He pulled out the phone book, trying to find a restaurant that wasn't a fast-food place. He was so tired of meals that came in a sack!

After some discussion they decided on a café that had burgers *and* vegetables.

"That Samantha is a bey-otch," Rachel said later as she dipped her onion ring in ketchup.

"What's a bee…whatever?" Hannah asked.

"It's not something you should repeat, punkin." It wasn't much of an explanation, but it was as good as she was going to get. "Rachel, what makes you say that?"

"Because she is." Her whine reminded him of fingernails on a blackboard.

Chad set his burger down and focused on his daughter. He had to nip this in the bud. "Tell you what. You're going to have to be around her a lot at the barn and at school, so why don't you reserve judgment until you get to know her better?"

Rachel took a big swallow of Coke. Chad knew stalling when he saw it, but at least she hadn't immediately shot down his idea.

"Okay." She stretched the word out like a rubber band. "But I know I'm right. She dresses like a rodeo slut and, even worse, she does all that cowboy crap."

"Rachel! I don't want to hear you talk like that about anyone. And what's with all this snobbery about English and Western riding? I don't get it."

She ignored the question. "Oh, fine. I won't say anything else about her."

That was probably the only concession she was going to make. And if Chad wanted an answer to his question about riding he'd have to ask someone else.

Then he remembered what he had in his pocket. "Look what I have." He held up the keys to their new home, hoping that would catch Rachel's attention. "While I was out running errands I went by the base housing office and picked them up."

"Can we go look at it after dinner?" Hannah asked.

"Sure, eat up and we'll head back to the base."

WHEN CHAD PULLED INTO THE driveway of their new home he almost swallowed his tongue. The house was a flat-roofed square brick building with a single carport. Not only was it tiny, it was so…so '60s. He had to admit he was stunned and apparently he wasn't the only one. The silence from the peanut gallery was deafening. Please God the inside was better than the outside. If it wasn't he was in a bunch of trouble.

Chad had decided to live on base so that Rachel and Hannah would have the stability of an extended military family and the safety of a controlled environment. As an added bonus he was hoping the neighborhood kids would make them welcome. That's the way things happened in the world of military brats.

"Let's not jump to any conclusions before we go in. I'm sure it'll be fine." Chad was trying to be enthusiastic. "Come on, guys, hop out. Chop-chop." Great. Now he sounded like a demented cheerleader.

"Oh, all right," Rachel whined.

Hannah, his little Energizer Bunny, skipped to the front door. "Come on, Daddy, let's see the inside." She was bouncing from one foot to the other. At least someone was excited about their new home. She was the first in the door, and the first to express disappointment.

"Daddy! This is so small."

Sixteen hundred square feet to be exact—not exactly palatial. Chad had known it would be a tight fit. He wasn't, however, prepared for the size of the rooms. The master bedroom could barely hold a king-size bed. He'd give it six weeks before they were out house hunting.

"Is this all there is?" Rachel asked as she wandered into one of the bedrooms. A second later she stuck her head out the door. "My closet in Virginia was bigger than this. Where am I going to put my furniture?"

That was a good question. This was going to be like fitting ten pounds of stuff into a five-pound box.

Hannah was wandering down the hall, peering into each doorway. "Where is it?" she asked with a frown.

"Where's what?"

"The basement or the upstairs."

"This is all there is."

She turned in a circle, looking baffled. "You mean, there isn't anything else?"

"Yep, punkin, afraid so."

Rachel plopped down on the tile floor. "I can't believe you dragged us across the country to live *here*."

Chad couldn't believe it, either. "It'll be okay. I promise. They're planning to build some new housing. When that's finished we can move there, or we can find something in town." That was one promise he knew he could keep. This had the signs of being the longest three years of his life.

"Once you get settled in school, everything's going to look different." He was crossing his fingers that *different* was synonymous with *good*.

"Tell you what, tomorrow morning we'll go to the mall to buy you some new clothes for your first day of class. And you can help me pick out some curtains and stuff to spiff this place up. What do you say?" Chad wasn't an expert on kids' fashions or decorating, and he'd rather be staked out over an anthill than go shopping, but sometimes a guy had to do what a guy had to do.

MEANWHILE, BACK AT THE Montgomerys' house, Kelbie was ready to throttle her kid. "Okay, what gives?"

"What do you mean?" Sam asked. She widened her eyes in the picture of innocence.

"Come on, Sam. Why were you so rude to Rachel Cassavetes? I've never seen you act like that before."

"Mommmm."

"Cut the whining." Kelbie's patience was wearing thin. "I want some facts."

Sam twisted the end of her ponytail, the way she always did when she was nervous. "Didn't you see how she pranced in with her fancy horse and hoity-toity clothes?"

There was that whine again.

"I'm from Virginia." Sam imitated Rachel's soft Southern drawl. "And I'm a princess."

"Samantha Jane Montgomery! I'm ashamed of you. She didn't do any of that."

"Yes, she did! That little snob thinks we're hicks from the sticks."

"How do you know what she was thinking? You two didn't say more than two words to each other." Kelbie was hoping that logic would work. She should've known better. That child was mule stubborn.

"I just know!"

Yep, a Missouri mule had nothing on her daughter.

Chapter Eight

Two days in temporary lodging were enough for Chad. So bright and early, they loaded up their stuff, grabbed breakfast at the on-base Burger King and headed to their new home. Today was not only moving day, it was also the first day of school. Rachel had flat out refused when he'd offered to walk her to the bus stop. Hannah, on the other hand, had cried all the way to the end of the block. It wasn't until she started a conversation with another girl her age that her tears dried up.

An unusual aspect of this assignment was the fact that Perry was managed by a private contractor. The Gen Tech Corporation was responsible for aircraft maintenance, simulator instruction and all other aspects of the base, excluding the flying mission. Because there weren't many upper level troops, both officers and enlisted, the number of teenagers on base was limited. Socially speaking, Hannah would be okay. But what about Rachel?

One worry at a time—right now Chad had a move to supervise.

The first of two moving vans was due any minute, so when Chad heard a knock at the door he was expecting a burly moving guy. Instead he found an attractive brunette holding a plate of chocolate-chip cookies.

"Hi, I'm Amy Decker. My husband is Dale Decker, the T-6 squadron commander. We live next door. I heard that your moving van is coming today so I thought you could use some munchies." She handed him the plate. "Did you know that you're the talk of the neighborhood?"

That wasn't surprising. Living on base was like being in a small town—very little was private, but if you needed a friend all you had to do was yell. It had been a long time since anyone had welcomed him with home-made goodies.

"I noticed your daughter sat with mine on the bus. Piper is the one with the pigtails. She's in the second grade. How about yours?" Amy's smile took her from moderately attractive to downright pretty.

"Hannah is a second grader, too." Chad was wondering if he should invite her in even without furniture when Amy graciously let him off the hook.

"I won't keep you any longer. I just wanted to tell you not to worry about a thing. Piper will take care of Hannah. I don't think my young'un ever met a stranger and she's quite a magpie. She's just like her daddy."

Amy was so friendly Chad was tempted to use her for a sounding board on some of his parenting questions, but he didn't even know the woman. What he wouldn't give for a mom or a sister or even a friend who could guide him through the minefield of the female psyche.

But he didn't have anyone, so somehow they'd muddle through. The big question was why didn't kids come with an owner's manual?

Thirty minutes later the first moving van arrived and deposited the ten thousand pounds of furniture he'd shipped from Germany. That shipment pretty much filled the house on its own. Then the second truck showed up with the kids' things and it was official—the house was bursting at the seams.

Chad glanced at his watch to see if it was time to meet Hannah's bus. Nope, he still had an hour in which to create order out of chaos. Boxes were stacked almost to the ceiling and furniture was pushed up against the walls. An hour—who was he kidding? If he managed to unearth the coffeepot and some sheets before he had to go to work next week it would be a miracle.

"Hey, Dad. Where are you?" Rachel called. She'd made him promise he wouldn't meet her at the bus. He remembered how important independence was for a teenager.

"In the kitchen." Chad stepped around a pile of boxes so his daughter could find him. "At least I think this is the kitchen. Right now I'm not sure about anything."

Rachel slowly spun around, taking in the moving-day bedlam. "How are we going to live here?"

"I guess we'll have to find a place for all this stuff. What do you think?"

She gave him her most eloquent "duh, Dad" look.

"How was school?"

Rachel shrugged. "Okay."

That was edifying. So Chad tried again. "Did you meet anyone?"

"A couple of people on the bus." Rachel made her way to the refrigerator. "Did you buy any snacks?"

Shopping, cleaning, unpacking, kids and a job—and to think that three months ago all he'd had to worry about was people shooting at him. "No, I had to wait around for the movers, and the phone and the cable company." He gave up on trying to pry open yet another box marked Kitchen. "But Mrs. Decker next door brought these." He handed Rachel the plate of cookies.

"As soon as you dump your stuff, we'll go to the bus stop to pick up Hannah. Then we can go to the commissary," he added. The on-base grocery store was kind of a cross between Costco and Safeway. "We have to stock up on the basics but we'll also get some goodies. We need some food in the house. What's on your shopping list?"

"Chocolate, lots of chocolate."

"We can do that."

That seemed to appease his eldest child. She wandered toward her bedroom and the next thing he knew she'd tossed an empty box into the hall.

Good. She was settling in, or at least unpacking her things. Now if Hannah got off the bus smiling they'd have it made.

Chad's prayers were answered when Hannah and her new best friend, Piper, hopped off the bus chattering a mile a minute.

"Daddy, this is Piper. She lives next door. Isn't that cool?"

"That certainly is cool." In fact, the kid was a godsend.

Amy had joined their group. "Why doesn't Hannah come over to play while you get organized?"

"That's fine with me." Having one less person along would make the shopping easier. "Punkin, do you want to go to Piper's house?"

Hannah and Piper answered with a chorus of squeals.

So with Rachel's help the milk and toilet paper hunt turned into a full-scale assault on the grocery aisles. They filled the cart with everything from soup to nuts.

Chad was stacking canned goods in the pantry when there was another knock at the door. This place was turning into Grand Central Station.

"Rachel, would you get that?" No answer. She was probably plugged in.

Chad abandoned his grocery duties and made his way

through the debris. This time his visitor was a man carrying a six-pack of beer. Chad couldn't be rude, could he?

"Come on in. You're exactly the person I wanted to see." At this point, Chad didn't care who the visitor was. He stepped aside to let him enter.

"I'm Dale Decker. I hear you've met the rest of my clan, Amy and Piper."

"I'm Chad Cassavetes." He put his hand out for a neighborly shake. "Good to meet you. And please tell me you're sharing that beer."

"I sure am." Dale plucked two bottles from the cardboard six-pack and popped the tops. "Here you go." He handed over one of the longnecks.

"Let me see if I can find a place for us to sit." Chad moved some boxes and cleared a spot at the bar separating the galley kitchen from the dining area.

"Daddy, I'm going to show Piper my room." Hannah and Piper arrived in a flurry of little girl chatter. It did Chad's heart good to see his daughter having fun. The girls skipped down the hall as if they'd known each other for years.

"I'm thrilled that Hannah has found a friend."

"Been there, done that," Dale agreed. He glanced around at the chaos. "I remember this. It's always tough. Before I forget, Amy sent me over to invite you guys to supper. Totally casual, hamburgers and hot dogs, but I can rustle up a couple more beers."

"That sounds great. What time do you want us?"

"Whatever works for you. We're not knee-deep in this." Dale didn't bother to hide his chuckle.

THE DECKERS' TINY LIVING ROOM was the mirror image of the Cassavetes' except it felt like a home. There were pictures on the walls, rugs on the floor and a calico cat nestled in a rocking chair. Amy handed Chad a bowl of chips to go along with the guacamole that was already on the table. "So, is Mrs. Cassavetes planning to join you?" Her interrogation was about as transparent as a piece of Saran Wrap.

Dale gave him a "what can I do" shrug.

Chad knew there were rumors floating around about his marital status, but he wasn't sure how much to share with his new neighbors. Knowing that rumors thrived on half-truths, he decided to tell them the whole story. He looked around to see what his girls were doing. Hannah was playing outside with Piper and Rachel was glued to a TV show.

"There isn't a Mrs. Cassavetes. This isn't for public consumption, but while I was in Afghanistan my ex-wife left the girls with her parents and took off to Central America. My father-in-law has Parkinson's and they couldn't take care of the kids. Not that I really wanted them to. So I finagled an assignment to the training command. That was the only way I felt I could make it as a single dad."

Amy and Dale gave each other a look that Chad recognized as nonverbal communication. It was a skill he and Lynn had never mastered. Amy was dying to ask for more details but Dale was telling her to drop it. She apparently listened and decided to change the subject.

"You realize you're going to be fair game for every matchmaker on base, don't you?" she asked. Actually, maybe he'd rather discuss Lynn.

"Amy!"

"Well, he is. More chips?" Amy didn't wait for an answer before she grabbed the empty bowl and marched back to the kitchen.

"That's okay. I'm sure it's true." Wasn't it interesting

that when he thought about dating he pictured a redheaded pixie named Kelbie? He'd known her only a couple of days and she was already on his mind.

"Sorry to say, it won't take long for the fact that you're divorced to hit the grapevine. And then everyone who knows a single woman of any age or description will be planning an introduction party," Dale said with a sympathetic shake of his head.

Chad took a long swig of beer. "I'm going to be too busy to date."

Dale grinned and Chad didn't know whether that meant he wasn't going to be busy or that he'd eventually succumb to the Perry AFB dating machine.

Amy returned with another round of guacamole and set it on the table. "Do you know what you need?"

"Whatever it is, don't listen to her," Dale said. This couple joked around but obviously had a relationship that was built on love and respect.

"We need to find you a nanny with a driver's license."

Amy was practically gloating, but she was right. A nanny was exactly what Chad needed. But how would he find someone who'd be willing to tote his kids hither and yon?

He helped himself to more dip. "I'm up for suggestions."

By now Amy was really getting into the spirit of things. "I hear all the time from student wives and the instructor pilots' wives that it's almost impossible to find a job. And if they don't have kids or an all-encompassing hobby, they get bored. I'll help you put out the word, and I bet you'll have your pick of people."

Chad looked to Dale for his opinion.

The man shot his wife a proud glance. "I'm sure it'll work. When Amy puts her mind to something, it gets done. She's a CPA so it goes with the job."

"That's impressive. I'll be even more impressed if you can find me a nanny." Chad could feel his tension ease. "I've spent some sleepless nights trying to figure out how to make everything work. Life as a single dad is not easy."

Chapter Nine

Kelbie's Saturdays were generally spent on errands, riding, barn work and trying to keep up with Sam. She had hired help for some of the mucking and feeding, but that didn't mean there wasn't still a lot to do.

"What's on your schedule for today, and do I have to drive you anywhere?" Kelbie was anxiously awaiting the day Samantha got her license. That was going to make life so much easier.

"Nothing special." Sam didn't bother to look up as she poured milk over her cereal. "Lonnie Roy wants me to go with him to the rodeo in Stillwater. Is that okay? A bunch of kids will be there."

Lonnie Roy was like a brother to Samantha, and Kelbie had known him since he was in diapers, *but* he was seventeen years old and consequently, his hormones were pinging out of control. Sort of like Kelbie's when she thought about Chad Cassavetes.

"Only if you get your barn chores done. And if you make sure you're home at a reasonable time." Too bad she couldn't send her daughter to a cloister. "When is your next drill team practice?"

"Tomorrow afternoon in Stillwater. I promise I'll be up

early to get everything done. So may I go to the rodeo, please, please?" She punctuated her request by clasping her hands beseechingly.

"Okay. Just remember your curfew."

Sam jumped up and kissed her mom's cheek. "Thank you," she yelled over her shoulder as she sprinted off with her cell phone already pressed to her ear.

When had her baby grown up? And how was Kelbie going to cope when she left home? That was a good question, and not something she wanted to dwell on. It had been just the two of them for so long, she didn't know what she'd do without Sam to take care of.

On that depressing note, Kelbie wandered out to the barn. Mucking stalls was a great way to meditate. She was halfway across the gravel lot that separated the barn from her fenced backyard when she spied Chad's truck.

Her heart actually skipped a beat, which annoyed the heck out of her. Sure, he was a good-looking guy, and he was certainly charming, but still…

Kelbie was so deep in thought she almost didn't notice him watching Hannah at the outdoor arena. He was leaning on the wooden fence, with one foot hooked on the bottom rung. The wind was blowing his sandy-blond hair and he was wearing the ever-present Oakley sunglasses.

"Hey, there." She mimicked his pose at the fence. "She's a good rider—and such a sweetheart."

He chuckled. "I agree with you on both counts."

"I see you got your truck fixed." Brilliant. Why couldn't she think of anything better to say?

"Thanks again for helping us. We'd probably still be out on the highway if you hadn't stopped." He grinned and Kelbie almost swooned.

What should she say now? *You're cute as a speckled*

pup, in a strictly macho kind of way? Good golly, no! Was she losing her mind? In a few years he'd finish his assignment and be on his way.

"Have you moved in?" Oh, goody, her chitchatting ability had kicked in again.

To Kelbie's surprise, he laughed. "Not so you could tell. We have boxes and stuff piled everywhere." He rested both arms on the top rail. "When I decided to live on base I didn't realize quite how cramped the quarters would be."

"I know. A friend of mine lived out there. We used to laugh about the size of the closets."

"The closets are the least of my problems. The master bathroom is so tiny I can barely turn around in it."

That wasn't surprising. He wasn't exactly a small guy.

"How do the girls like it here?"

"It's too early to tell, but I have my fingers crossed. I hope the riding helps them make a quick adjustment."

Kelbie nodded. "You know how it is with girls and their horses." She was still wondering where Rachel and Hannah's mom was, especially considering Chad wasn't wearing a ring and he didn't have a tan line indicating anything recent. But again, why did she care?

KELBIE MONTGOMERY WOULD BE a terrible spy. Chad had to smother a laugh at the unsubtle way she checked out his ring finger.

"How long have you been a single dad?" He'd give her an A for effort. She didn't bother with the preliminaries. Instead she went straight to the heart of the matter.

"Not long. A couple of months." Although his answer could have meant almost anything, she obviously assumed the worst. Much to his surprise, she took his hand. And he was even more astonished by how right it felt.

"I'm so sorry. That had to be awful."

Chad shook his head, hoping to jettison some of the lustful thoughts that were racing through his brain. "What did you say?"

She gave him a strange look. "Losing your wife must have been terrible."

Chad had to correct that assumption. "Lynn's alive and, uh, I guess she's well." How much should he tell Kelbie? He really didn't know her but sensed he could trust her.

"We divorced five years ago, and since I was gone a lot, Lynn got primary custody of the kids. When I was in Afghanistan, she became involved with a guy my in-laws described as skanky." Chad shrugged. "I was blown away that they even knew the word. At any rate, she left everything, including our kids, and went off to Central America with him. She told her mom she needed to find herself."

"Was she lost?" Kelbie scoffed. "What a crock."

"That was my sentiment exactly." The more he got to know Kelbie Montgomery, the more he enjoyed her—and wanted to see her in nothing but a grin and a blush. Oh, boy, that kind of thinking had to come to a halt, pronto. He had way too much on his plate to even consider dating.

"You don't know where she is?"

"Not precisely." If Kelbie had even an inkling of what he was thinking she'd be hauling butt across the pasture. He might not be able to partake, but he could certainly look. "I hired a private investigator and he tracked her to Belize. According to him, this Leonard Schmidt character bought some land in the rain forest and that seems to be where they're living. I just thank God she didn't take Hannah and Rachel with her."

Kelbie put her hand over her wonderfully kissable mouth. "That would've been horrible. It almost sounds like Jim Jones and all those poor people who drank that poisoned punch." She apparently realized that her remark wasn't exactly tactful. "I mean…"

Her face turned bright red, fueling his fantasies of a blushing Kelbie. *You lech!* She was trying to make conversation and he was mentally undressing her.

"Believe me, the thought has crossed my mind, too, so don't worry about it."

Chad acknowledged that his social skills were rusty, but discussing his ex—and her foibles—with a woman he barely knew wasn't even close to smooth. Not that it mattered. Cute little Kelbie didn't seem to think of him as anything other than a client.

Chapter Ten

Monday mornings at the Chamber of Commerce were normally hectic, and with only two weeks left until the October Wheatland Rodeo and Horse Show, the situation was more frenetic than usual. Part of Kelbie's job was to co-coordinate the horse show and consequently she was stressed to the max. Thank goodness someone else was responsible for the rodeo. But somehow she still had time to think about a certain tall, blond and handsome air force officer. Funny how that worked.

"Hey, boss. You have a call." Sherry was the Chamber's receptionist, as well as Kelbie's friend. She pointed at the cordless phone she was holding against her almost nonexistent chest, and grimaced. "Loynelle Baumgartner. She insists on speaking to you right this minute."

Kelbie would rather eat Rocky Mountain oysters than deal with this charter member of the Horse Show Association. The old biddy was a royal, raging pain in the butt. "Okay. I'll deal with her," she whispered. She drew in a fortifying breath and took the phone. "Hi, Loynelle. What's up?"

"What's up? What do you mean, *what's up?*" the woman screeched.

Kelbie glared at the receiver, causing Sherry to break into giggles.

"What can I do for you this fine fall morning?"

Loynelle had a gravelly, cigarette-tinged voice that brought to mind bad dye jobs and pursed lips. "We have to discuss the final plans for the big show."

"What specifically would you like to talk about?" Kelbie asked in her best "I'm running for student body president" voice.

"You're not really gonna have jumping contests with those darned English saddles, are you? That's…that's just not right."

Cowboy hard-liners were of the opinion that English riding was nothing more than little girls in hard hats prancing their ponies around a ring. They also believed in the inherent superiority of the sturdy Western equipment that was designed for hours in the saddle, punchin' cows. To their way of thinking, a Western saddle was a La-Z-Boy for the back of a horse. English saddles were originally created for European cavalry horses so they were small and supple.

"Yes, ma'am. That's exactly what we're going to do." Kelbie was practicing her PR skills, when in reality she wanted to let Loynelle have it with both barrels. Not only was the woman seriously biased, she had no right to tell Kelbie how to do her job. For now she'd keep that opinion to herself. "Do you have an objection?"

"It's just not natural, that's all."

"Not natural?" Kelbie was tempted to stomp over to the real estate office that Loynelle owned with her husband, and snatch the woman bald-headed. Fortunately, sanity prevailed.

Kelbie took a deep breath before she spoke again. "If you remember, I'm also on the board of directors of the association, and my students *are* going to compete, regardless of whether you think it's 'natural' or not. And I'm sure there are many parents in this town who will agree with me." Some of them could buy and sell small countries. And their Oklahoma roots went back to the land rush. All of which Loynelle knew.

"Don't get your knickers in a twist. I was merely suggesting—"

"Tell you what," Kelbie interrupted. "Let's call this one a draw and get on with planning the show."

"Humph. I'll be at the meeting on Tuesday," Loynelle said before hanging up. That was a clear indication she realized she was out of luck.

"See you there," Kelbie chirped, even though the line was dead.

"That sounded like a barrel of fun," Sherry stated.

"Did you know you're a nosy Nellie?" Kelbie blew her friend a raspberry. That was a throwback to their days in junior high school.

"And proud of it. How do you think I stay on top of everything that goes on around here? I live to keep you out of trouble. Speaking of trouble, I understand there's a good-looking man hanging around the barn."

Darn that Marge's hide! Was nothing around here private? "He's a client."

"So why are you blushing?"

"Daddy, Miss Marge told me there's a horse show the weekend after next and if I want to I can do one of the small jumping courses." Hannah was so excited she was dancing in place.

"What kind of small course?" Horse lingo was like a foreign language to Chad.

"I don't know. They're sort of this high." She held her chubby hands about a foot apart.

"If Miss Marge thinks you're ready, I'm sure it will be fine."

The Cassavetes family was barely a week into their adventure and they'd already experienced a world of change. The girls were in new schools and, thankfully, seemed to be fitting in. And the horses appeared to be happy in their new barn.

As for what was happening in Chad's life, between getting the kids off to school in the morning and supervising homework at night, occasionally mucking stalls and participating in the mandatory and exhausting social schedule that was an integral part of his job, he was a busy guy. He still thought about Kelbie, but he barely had time to breathe, much less date.

Amy had scored on the nanny hunt with an instructor pilot's wife. The chauffeuring duties had been handed off to Stacy Kowalski and her chartreuse VW. Even Rachel thought the car was cool, and that was saying a lot.

Life in their household was slowly, but surely, getting back on an even keel. It had taken a while to find the plates and silverware, and if Chad never ordered another pizza he'd be a very happy man, but all in all things were going pretty well.

That wasn't to say everything was hunky-dory. For instance, fixing a seven-year-old girl's hair was a daunting task. Her ponytail was always either too tight or too loose. Flying a fingertip formation was a piece of cake compared to pleasing Hannah.

Thank goodness Rachel could fix her own hair. With her it was a whole different set of problems—all typical of a teen in a new environment.

On the plus side, she'd found a friend. The problem was

that her new buddy was a seventeen-year-old boy she'd met at the barn. Lately all Chad heard was Colin did this and Colin did that. Rachel said he was coaching her. What did that mean? For adults, a two-year age gap didn't make much difference, but when it came to teenagers it was an abyss.

So Chad finally succumbed to his curiosity and called Kelbie, hoping she'd give him the straight skinny on this Colin kid. Chad trusted Rachel, but remembered being a seventeen-year-old boy himself, and that made him very cautious. Luckily, Kelbie agreed to meet him at the Wagon Wheel Barbecue for lunch.

"I'm glad you found this place," she said as she rushed in, followed by a gust of wind. "I know it's out of the way, but they have the best brisket you've ever tasted."

Being a Southern boy, Chad was more familiar with pulled pork, but barbecue in any form was okay with him. "Your directions were perfect."

"Good." She grabbed the menu that was stuck between the Tabasco and the ketchup. "I'm starving."

Chad watched with amazement as the five-foot-nothing dynamo plowed through a combo plate like a blitzing line-backer through a bad offensive line in a football game.

"Mmm, that was fantastic," she said, dabbing her face with a paper napkin when she'd finished.

A guy would have to be brave or awfully foolish to try and sneak chow off *her* plate, but it was refreshing to see a woman who enjoyed her food. Chad was also mesmerized by the spot of BBQ sauce she'd missed at the corner of her mouth. What would she do if he reached over and wiped it off?

He'd been through combat, so he decided to chance it. He dabbed at the brown smudge. "Barbecue sauce," he said, right before he licked his finger clean.

Chapter Eleven

A cold front had whipped through the Oklahoma plains on Friday night. That proved to be a mixed blessing. The stifling postsummer heat was broken, but the crisp autumn air inspired even the calmest horse to be as skittish as an unbroken foal.

"Daddy, are you staying for the whole show?" Hannah asked from the backseat of the truck as they drove to the barn.

"I sure am. How do you think you and Patches would get home otherwise?"

She was being a little chatterbox. On the other hand, Rachel was abnormally quiet. Chad wasn't sure what she had up her sleeve, but he did know it had something to do with the duffel bag stored at her feet. He hoped it wouldn't be anything too outrageous, but when it came to kids all bets were off.

When Chad pulled up to the barn he noticed Kelbie supervising a group of kids who were wrapping their horses' legs. The way that lady filled out a pair of Wranglers was impressive, but he couldn't believe what he'd done at lunch the other day. Chad wasn't in the market for a date or anything else, but he had to admit she was the only woman who had managed to snag his attention in a *very* long time.

Rachel and Hannah were out of the truck almost before he turned off the ignition.

"Miss Kelbie, we're here," Hannah squealed.

"So I see." Kelbie patted the exuberant child's shoulder. "Why don't you get your pony ready? He wants to be pretty. Hi, Chad," she continued. "As soon as everyone's finished we'll get going. You might want to get your rig hooked up so you can follow us to the fairground."

Was she as blasé about him as she seemed, or was she just a good actress? Chad had never backed away from a challenge, but this situation was different. Pursuing Kelbie Montgomery, hometown girl extraordinaire, could prove devastating.

KELBIE COULDN'T THINK straight when Lt. Col. Cassavetes was around. But there he was in his faded jeans, an equally washed-out polo shirt and scuffed boots. That boy was a cowgirl's little slice of heaven. But this cowgirl had been there, done that and was never, ever going to make that mistake again.

The next time Harlan Kendrick asked her out, she was going to accept. Good old Harlan owned the feed lot, and you couldn't get much safer than someone who fattened cattle for a living.

"Yes, ma'am. I'll get on it right away." Chad saluted.

Huh? In all her musings she'd forgotten what they were discussing. Oh, that's right. He was talking about joining the caravan to the fairgrounds.

"Mom, where's my saddle pad? I can't find it anywhere," Sam announced. She looked frazzled, but remembered her manners when she spied Chad. "Hi, Mr. Cassavetes. Is this your first rodeo?"

"I went to the professional rodeo out in Vegas. Does that count?" he asked with a grin.

Man, that smile of his was adorable. *Cut it out!* Kelbie told herself. That kind of thinking was dangerous and she'd darn sure better remember it.

"Has Rachel ever been to a rodeo?"

Sam's question seemed innocent, but Kelbie wasn't fooled for a moment. The girls' relationship hadn't improved from that very first day. If she didn't miss her guess, Sam was intimidated by Rachel's East Coast sophistication. And she suspected something similar was going on with Rachel.

She wished she could knock their heads together or lock them in a room without snacks or their iPods until they called a truce.

"I don't think they have many rodeos in Virginia," Chad said.

"Oh?" Samantha looked confused by his answer, but apparently decided to press on with more compelling issues.

"Mom." She elongated that single syllable into three. "I need my saddle pad."

"I washed it last night. It's in the laundry room."

"Thanks." Sam kissed Kelbie's cheek and gave Chad a quick wave before sprinting to the house.

"Hey." Kelbie glanced at her watch. "I'd better get a move on or we'll be late." As an exit line, that wasn't very inspired, but too bad.

Her anxiety was silly. Why would anyone that good-looking be interested in a single mom with freckles who blushed at the drop of a hat? The answer was simple. He wouldn't.

CHAD WATCHED AS KELBIE deftly backed her truck up to a huge gooseneck trailer. Even with a spotter it usually took him a couple of tries—and a whole lot of cussing—to get his pickup positioned correctly. But one try and she had it made. Chad had offered to help, even though she was perfectly capable of doing it herself. It was a guy thing to want to assist the little lady. And if he dared say that out loud he'd probably get smacked.

Kelbie jumped down from her truck and wiped her hands on a most delectable derriere. None of the women he'd dated—particularly not the one he'd married—would be caught dead smearing grease on their designer jeans.

"Oops." Kelbie raised her hands. "My mom used to yell at me for doing stuff like that. The way I figure it, after a day at the horse show everything will be toxic, so why not start early?" She laughed at her own wit. "Do you need some help getting hooked up?"

Oh, yes, but did he really want to show her his incompetence? "Sure, why not?"

THE LOGISTICS OF MOVING kids, horses, equipment and food across town were akin to pulling off an invasion, Kelbie imagined—except that military types didn't have to deal with tears, teen distress and reluctant equines. Everyone was finally in the right place and being handled by their own parents—with some help from barn staff. Most of the moms and dads were veterans of the amateur horse show circuit. Not Chad Cassavetes. He was so totally out of his element that it would've been funny if he wasn't so darn sexy.

"Kelbie, I have something of a problem." During the last couple of weeks he'd learned a lot about the care and feeding of a pony, but today he was having trouble.

"The stubborn little cuss is refusing to get out of the trailer," he said with a huff.

The poor man still had so far to go. "Let me help." In

about five seconds Patches was out of the trailer, and Chad was calmer.

"Thanks." He ran his finger lightly down Kelbie's cheek. "You had a smudge of dirt on your face," he explained a sheepish grin. "Looks like I'm doing that a lot lately."

Just the touch of his finger sent a jolt all the way to the tips of her toes. Oh, please, please, please save her from this temptation.

THE WHEATLAND COUNTY FAIRGROUND was the only place in the county that had facilities appropriate for both rodeo and equestrian competitions. Since the rodeo folks had staked out all the stalls, everyone else had to tie their horses to their trailers. Kelbie and Chad were parked side by side.

"*Daddy,* I can do it," Hannah griped. She was trying to attach Patches's lead rope to the back of the trailer, but she was too short.

Chad was reaching for the rope when a beater truck backfired on its way by.

Patches jerked so fast Hannah lost her grip on the rope, and the pony was gone, sprinting straight toward the highway. The stirrups were flopping against his sides, inciting even more terror. If he found the gate, that poor animal was going to be roadkill.

"*Daddy!*" Hannah screamed.

Chad was off like an Olympic sprinter. He couldn't possibly catch that horse, but Kelbie had to applaud the effort—even if it was fueled by desperation.

"Stay right here," Kelbie told Hannah as she grabbed a bucket of grain and flagged down a passing cowboy.

"Give me a leg up and head toward that bay pony." She handed him the bucket and put her foot in the stirrup where his foot had previously been.

"Yes, ma'am." He grabbed her hand and pulled her on board. "Charlie," he yelled to a buddy a few feet away. "See that pony over there? We need to round him up."

"Gotcha," Charlie responded.

"Don't scare him," Kelbie warned. Cowboys weren't exactly known for their finesse.

They galloped past Chad. He was fast, but not as speedy as a panicked horse whose first instinct was flight.

Fortunately, Patches didn't spy the exit, and halted next to a fence. His head drooped and his sides were huffing like overworked bellows.

"Let me off here!" Kelbie yelled.

Realizing that quarter horses could stop on a dime, she grabbed the cowboy's waist and held on tight. Kelbie hoped like heck she wouldn't fall on her rump. *That* would be the talk of the county.

Mission accomplished. She slid down and walked toward the terrified pony, shaking the feed bucket and making cooing noises.

Chad caught up with her and bent over, trying to catch his breath. It was hard to tell who'd had the worst end of this deal—man or beast.

"Patches, lookie, lookie. I have food," Kelbie said in the singsong voice she used when she trained young foals.

As she shook the feed bucket Patches took a tentative step forward, proving there wasn't an iota of difference between a guy and a pony. All you had to do was discover their weakness and go for it. In the case of a horse, that was through his stomach. Come to think of it, that worked for men, too.

Patches took another step and then another, until Kelbie was able to grab his halter. Thank God! The thought of telling that sweet little girl her best friend was dead gave her chills. Kelbie rubbed the pony's velvet muzzle. "Were you scared?"

"I don't know about him, but I certainly was," Chad admitted.

"Me, too. I'm sure Hannah's hysterical by now."

He sighed. "This daddy duty is gonna do me in."

What could she say to that? Even at the best of times single parenthood was tough. Chad and the girls were in a totally new environment, which would make it worse. Coming from Virginia, the Cassavetes family probably felt as if they'd been transported to a foreign country.

She and Chad were leading Patches toward the trailer when Kelbie heard one of the cowboys mutter, "Sure as shootin' that damned English saddle spooked him. It just ain't normal."

She coughed to hide her chuckle. Some things never changed, especially when hardheaded cowpokes were part of the equation.

Chapter Twelve

"I'm not going to ride!" Hannah slammed her hands on her tiny hips. Considering she'd seen Patches haul butt as if he had a pack of wolves on his tail, this announcement wasn't too surprising.

"Come on, Hannah. Don't chicken out now. It'll be fine, really it will." Rachel was trying her best to be encouraging.

"I don't want to." Hannah's pout said it all.

Chad felt there was an important lesson to be learned, about not letting fear control her life. "Patches was scared. That's why he ran. He won't do that when you're on him. He loves you."

"You promise?"

"I can't promise. But I honestly don't think he will. Is that good enough?" Chad lifted Hannah's chin to look her in the eye.

"I'm scared."

"I know. It makes your tummy feel funny, doesn't it?"

She gave a small nod and started wringing her hands.

Chad's own stomach twisted seven ways from Sunday. "I get frightened in the cockpit sometimes, but it doesn't keep me from flying. The secret is to take a deep breath and press on."

Hannah squared her shoulders. "Okay, Daddy. I can do it. I will!"

That was his girl! At least one of them felt better. Why hadn't someone told him that a kid's horse show could be so terrifying?

Now that that was settled, the only blip on the day was Rachel and her buddy Colin's riding exhibition. It was choreographed to rap music and the two ruffians had dressed as the Blues Brothers. So that was what was in the secret duffel bag—a black hat, a black tie and sunglasses.

Kelbie had told him that Colin was the hottest young rider in western Oklahoma. He'd been to the McClay National Championship in Pennsylvania, and that was the zenith of the young hunter jumper world. In other words he was a really big dog in a very small kennel. Kelbie thought he had a girlfriend in Tulsa, but she wasn't sure.

The audience reaction to the exhibition was generational. The old-timers didn't get it. Everyone else, including Chad, thought it was funny. However, he couldn't laugh at Rachel's obvious adoration of her riding partner. That first crush was tough, especially if it was unrequited. From watching their interaction, Chad thought that was the case. And to that he said fantastic.

BY THE END OF THE DAY Chad was hot, tired and filthy. What made it worse was that Kelbie had the audacity to say this was par for the course.

"Congratulations, you've survived your first horse show. Are you ready to saddle up and mosey home?"

For sure!

"We're taking a bunch of kids to the Dairy Queen for ice cream. Do you and the girls want to go with us?"

"Can we, Daddy, can we?" Hannah pleaded. The kid

had clearly learned the art of supplication from her sister. "I really, really want a Peanut Buster Parfait."

"Yeah, that'd be cool," Rachel agreed. Although she was speaking to Chad she was looking at Colin.

A Butterfinger Blizzard did sound mighty good. "Sure."

It was a dusty and fragrant crew that marched into the ice cream parlor.

The woman behind the counter greeted them with a big smile and an impressive poof hairdo. "What can I do for you?"

There was an explosion of noise as each kid tried to answer at once. Until Marge let out a whistle that would make a pro football umpire jealous.

"One at a time," she instructed. "Try to act like young ladies. Except you, Colin."

By the time Chad reached the front of the line he could almost taste the combination of ice cream and candy. But before Miss DQ handed him his order she decided to do an impromptu advertisement.

"Ya know, you can turn this puppy upside down and it's so thick it'll stay put." To prove her point she flipped the cup over. Ice cream promptly fell out, making a mess of Chad's sneakers.

"Oops," she said as she leaned across the counter. "It's never done that before. I'll be darned."

Kelbie snorted and broke into a belly laugh. "I am so sorry. It's not funny." She slapped a hand over her mouth, trying to stifle her giggles. "Really." But the fact that she continued to laugh betrayed her true thoughts.

The kids were gathered around, staring at the puddle of ice cream.

"Sorry about that, sir. What else can I get for ya? On the house."

Kelbie had tears running down her cheeks from laughing so hard.

"Tell you what. Give me a banana split and two spoons," Chad answered. "The lady and I will share."

He understood the intimacy of sharing a dessert, and considering Kelbie's deer-in-the-headlights look, so did she. He wasn't sure what they had going, and flirting with her was probably a really bad idea. But sometimes a guy had to take a chance.

CHAD DIPPED HIS SPOON into the hot fudge, never taking his eyes off her. Then he slowly licked the spoon. Was it hot in here or was she the only one sweating like a marathon runner? Surely the air conditioner was on the fritz. But Kelbie would be damned if she fanned her face.

"You should try the vanilla." He helped himself to a mouthful of ice cream. "It's creamy and smooth." His voice was an aphrodisiac. And when he added a wink Kelbie almost melted on the spot. "And don't you love the cherry? Too bad there's only one. Would you like to share?" Chad took a nibble of the maraschino cherry and held out the other half.

She fought the urge to shut her eyes and cover her ears. Was it possible to have an orgasm simply by watching a guy eat? Thank God the kids were busy doing their own thing.

Kelbie knew this was all her own fault. If she hadn't laughed at Chad, she wouldn't be involved in this chocolatey version of foreplay.

"No," she squeaked, and then cleared her throat. "No thanks." She picked up her plastic spoon and delved into the caramel end of the sundae. Anything to stay as far away from his end as possible.

Chapter Thirteen

"Looks like you got some sun this weekend," Dale said as he poured a cup of coffee from the industrial-size urn located in the snack bar the two flying squadrons shared.

"The girls were in a horse show this weekend, so I've been officially indoctrinated into the cowboy world," Chad replied.

His neighbor stirred a liberal dollop of cream into his coffee. "The way I heard it, that horse show is a taste of the Wild West."

"It was an experience," Chad agreed. The most interesting part had been watching Kelbie Montgomery. Tiny as she was, she made wrangling a twelve-hundred-pound horse look easy, not to mention manhandling that behemoth truck. And the way she blushed when she was embarrassed was even more intriguing.

Yes, he had been flirting with her. And yes, he knew he shouldn't have. But it was fun, and it gave Chad hope that she wasn't as oblivious to him as she pretended.

"A word to the wise," Dale muttered.

The fact that his friend was almost whispering caught Chad's attention, and put an end to his more lustful thoughts. It was just as well. He didn't have the time, or the energy, to pursue a relationship.

"See the guy by the snack bar?" Dale was hiding behind his coffee cup.

Chad started to turn.

"Don't look!"

What was this, *Get Smart?*

"Do it subtly or he'll know I'm talking about him."

"Ooh-kay." Chad *subtly* reached for the cream. "Do you mean the foreign student?" he asked out the corner of his mouth. Maxwell Smart didn't have a thing to worry about.

"Yep, you need to watch out for him." His neighbor was barely moving his lips. "That's Lieutenant Ahvad Gavor. He's the biggest pain in the rear we've had in a long time. His daddy is a kingpin in the government of one of our 'friends.'" He emphasized the last word with finger quotations.

"He barely made it through the T-6 program and now he's yours. Watch out for him. Not only does he have an attitude, he's dangerous." Dale's T-6 program was the initial flight instruction. After completing that course of study aspiring fighter jocks went on to Chad's T-38 squadron. And if they got through that, they earned their silver wings.

Chad nodded, understanding everything his friend wasn't saying. The lieutenant had been a problem from the very beginning and he'd only made it this far because of his old man's influence. And now he was Chad's problem. If his existing headaches weren't enough, he was about to have a prima donna on his hands. *Whoopie!*

"Thanks for the heads-up."

Chad's job as squadron commander required a combination of talent and skill. He had to be a manager, an organizer, a pilot, a mediator and a schmoozer. He had students from every branch of the military, both American and foreign allies, under his command. In addition, he was responsible for the day-to-day work of the T-38 instructor pilots. It was a demanding but satisfying job. But all those positives had to have a few negatives—including students like Lt. Gavor.

"You're planning to go to all the graduation shindigs, aren't you?" Dale asked.

"Yep, I'll be there." The social engagements were an integral part of Chad's job and graduation weekends were particularly hectic. The pin-on ceremony was held during duty hours, but the formal graduation dinner was a night-time function. And considering there was a graduation every three weeks, that was a lot of socializing.

"With all the things we're expected to attend, I some-times feel like I spend more time with you guys than I do with my kid," Dale groused.

"You got that one right," Chad agreed.

IN HER POSITION WITH the Chamber of Commerce, Kelbie had attended several pilot training graduation dinners, but there was something different about this one. Could it be the tall, handsome man across the room? This was busi-ness, not pleasure, so she had to keep that in mind. And where had the word *pleasure* come from?

"Are you sure they're old enough to be pilots?" Sherry asked as she surveyed the new graduates. "They look like they're still in high school."

Kelbie had coerced her friend into being her date for the graduation dinner. After that flirtation at the Dairy Queen, she wasn't convinced she could face Chad alone.

"But, boy, oh, boy, are they good-looking," Sherry ob-served.

Yes, the young men in their formal mess dress uniforms— the air force version of a tuxedo—were handsome, but they didn't hold a candle to Lt. Col. Cassavetes.

"Is that the guy you picked up on the road?"

Busted! Kelbie hadn't realized she was staring. Heaven help her if Sherry caught wind of this attraction. That woman was like a pit bull with ham hock, especially when it came to matchmaking.

"Which one?" Kelbie tried to look innocent, but knew she was failing miserably.

"You're interested. You can't fool me." Her friend punctuated her assertion with a pointed finger.

"I'm not interested!"

"Oh, yes, you are. I know interested when I see it. Holy moley, this is good!"

"Ladies." There was no mistaking that voice.

"If you say anything you're dead." Kelbie muttered her warning before turning to face the man in question.

"Hi, Chad. Have you recovered from the horse show?" That was a safe topic—friendly but not very personal. At least it had nothing to do with banana splits and thoughts of hot sex.

"I think so."

"I have to apologize for losing it at the Dairy Queen. Once I started laughing I couldn't seem to stop."

"That's okay. I thought it was funny, too. I particularly enjoyed the banana split." His grin was absolutely lascivious.

Kelbie's face was so hot she was surprised she hadn't set off the fire alarm. Sharing ice cream with him was like sex without the finale.

There was a short pause in the conversation and then Sherry jumped in. "Are you going to introduce me?"

"Sure. Chad, this is Sherry. She works with me at the Chamber and we've been best friends since the first grade. I bribed her into coming to the dinner with me. Sherry, this is Chad Cassavetes, the new T-38 squadron leader."

"Miss Sherry." Chad took her hand. "It's nice to meet you. So you're Kelbie's date?"

"Uh, yeah," Sherry joked. "I made her beg before I gave in."

"I would've paid money to see that." His suggestive smile set Kelbie's knees to knocking. Darn it, she was experienced with cocktail party prattle, so why couldn't she chat up the guy with the Paul Newman eyes?

"Are you having a good time?" Chad sounded as if he was repeating himself.

Sherry jabbed her in the ribs. "What?" Kelbie had missed the gist of the conversation while she was fantasizing about his eyes.

"Oh, yeah. Sure." She could feel the heat slowly creeping up her neck again.

Her reaction to him was so out of character that she wasn't quite sure what was happening. It was like a roller coaster. There were lots of ups and downs. At times she felt like a kid with a first crush, and at others she was assaulted by purely adult lust. This attraction was disturbing on so many levels, but Kelbie's biggest fear was that she might be falling for him. And she'd say it again—that was *not* going to happen. Just the thought of him intruding in her nice safe environment was stomach turning.

Chapter Fourteen

It was Monday afternoon and Kelbie was still thinking about her recent encounter with Lt. Col. Chad Cassavetes. The way that man filled out a uniform was enough to give her heart palpitations. And that kind of thinking had to come to a halt. Mucking stalls was a great time to contemplate the world. And there was only one thing on Kelbie's mind: Lt. Col. Chad Cassavetes. She was really fighting this attraction, but so far she wasn't having much success.

His demeanor and take-charge attitude reminded her of Jason, but that was where the similarities ended. So obviously she wasn't attempting to replace her husband. But could she go into a relationship knowing it was only temporary?

Her musing was interrupted by a caterwauling from the arena. The words were indecipherable—she could hear only screeching and screaming—but Kelbie knew instantly who was responsible.

Couldn't someone else please take care of it? She propped her muck rake against the wall, praying the noise would cease, but no such luck. She was going to have to be the peacemaker.

Kelbie peeked into the arena. Samantha and Rachel

were rolling in the dirt and clawing at each other. This wasn't a kids' brawl with lots of noise and little action. What in bloody hell did they think they were doing?

"Stop it right this minute!" Kelbie shouted. A couple of students who had been watching the spectacle in amazement skittered off like cockroaches.

It was sheer luck that Kelbie was able to grab Samantha's T-shirt and Rachel's jeans to pull them apart.

"What in the Sam Hill is goin' on?" Marge hollered as she jumped the half door that led from the office to the indoor arena. She snagged Rachel and shot her a glare that would quell the most hardened felon. And she'd had lots of practice. In her previous career she'd been a guard at the Oklahoma State Prison in McAlester.

Kelbie pulled Sam to her feet and went nose to nose with her recalcitrant offspring. "Not a word, do you hear me? Not until I tell you to speak." She'd never been this mad, or disappointed, before.

Chad's daughter had a cut above her eyebrow and blood was streaming down her face. "Marge, why don't you take Rachel into the tack room and get her cleaned up? Samantha Jane, you come with me." Fully expecting her daughter to follow, Kelbie marched toward the bleachers at the end of the arena.

She wouldn't have been surprised if steam had been pouring out of her ears. She stomped up the steps and pointed to a wooden bench. "Sit! Now, what in blue blazes were you were doing out there?" Kelbie was trying to keep her cool but it wasn't easy.

"She asked for it," Samantha muttered.

"Don't start with that," Kelbie snapped. What had happened to the sweet girl her daughter used to be?

"Well, she did." This time the teen added a pout.

"I'm not going to listen to excuses. If you're not going to tell me everything, just stay here and do not move a muscle."

Kelbie stomped to the office, grabbed the cordless phone and flipped through the Rolodex, looking for Chad Cassavetes's emergency contact number.

"Lieutenant Colonel Cassavetes here."

"It's Kelbie. You need to come to the barn. We have a situation."

The minute the words were out of her mouth she realized she'd made a mistake. "Don't panic. Rachel and Sam got into a scuffle but no one's hurt. At least not yet. But I definitely think you need to drive out here."

"I'll be there in fifteen minutes."

CHAD'S HEART HAD ALMOST stopped when he got that call. Kelbie had said no one was hurt, but what the hell was going on? Rachel and Sam were in a fight? He raced up the gravel drive to the barn. No cop cars, no ambulance and no fire truck—that was good. So what was the emergency? He'd ditched an important meeting to hurry across town.

"Colonel Cassavetes, over here."

Colonel? What happened to calling him Chad? He followed the voice to the bleachers at one end of the ring, where Kelbie and her daughter were glaring at each other.

"Marge, would you guys come out here?" she yelled.

Chad was astonished when he saw his daughter. Rachel had blood on her T-shirt, her ponytail was at half-mast and dirt was smeared all down her face.

"What happened to you?" He was trying not to shout, but it was a losing battle.

Rachel pointed toward the bleachers. "*She* happened to me."

CHAD FELT AS IF HE'D BEEN sucked into a black hole. When the adults tried to question them, the girls had clammed up. As far as he knew Rachel was one step away from juvie. The ride home was the longest fifteen minutes in his life.

Hannah and Stacy were waiting on the front porch when Chad pulled into the driveway.

"Go to your room," he told Rachel. "Don't stop to talk to your sister. And if you slam the door, you're going to regret it. Do you understand?"

Rachel jumped from the pickup and ran into the house without saying a word.

"Colonel Cassavetes, I'm so sorry," Stacy said. "Mrs. Montgomery called and told me what happened. I should've stayed at the barn." The nanny was wringing her hands. "Hannah had to work on a project and Rachel said she'd be okay. I was planning to pick her up later."

"Don't worry, Stacy, none of this is your fault. Why don't you go on home? I have it covered."

"Yes, sir." She grabbed her purse and was out the door almost before he finished his sentence. Chad certainly couldn't blame her. He wished he could leave. The Cassavetes household had turned into a zoo.

He *really* didn't need this today. The meeting he'd jettisoned concerned the troublesome foreign student, Lt. Ahvad Gavon. It was going down just as Dale had predicted. According to his instructors the kid was an accident waiting to happen, but the powers that be at headquarters weren't willing to go up against his daddy's embassy. So they were stuck with him for at least another cycle. Chad hoped the guy didn't kill himself—or even worse, someone else.

But right now Chad's primary concern had to be Rachel.

He rubbed the bridge of his nose, hoping his burgeoning headache would go away.

"What happened, Daddy?" He hadn't seen Hannah follow him inside.

"Rachel did a bad thing today and I need to talk to her. Why don't you run next door to the Deckers'? I'll come get you in a few minutes."

He waited until she was outside before he picked up the phone to explain the situation to Amy. Knowing his neighbor, he figured she'd treat Hannah to a hearty dose of cookies and sympathy.

And then it really hit him. In the good times and the bad, he was all alone. God help him.

Chad poured a glass of orange juice, wishing it could be a single malt whiskey on the rocks. But he needed his wits about him for what he was about to do. He took a deep breath and marched to Rachel's room.

She was facedown on her bed. He couldn't tell if she was crying, or even worse, trying not to cry. Chad didn't know where to start.

Rachel mumbled something unintelligible against her pillow.

Chad ran his hand across her silky hair. He'd missed so much of his daughters' young lives, and even as hard as these teenage years appeared to be, he planned to relish every minute of his time with them. Well, maybe not *every* minute.

"What did you say?"

She rolled over and gave him a look every parent had seen at least once—the one that indicated you'd just dropped at least thirty IQ points.

"I said I'm sorry." She sniffed. "And I really, really am."

"Why don't you sit up? I'll be right back." Chad retreated to the bathroom to get a wet washcloth. He couldn't have a serious discussion with her when she looked as if she'd been in a gang fight.

He handed her the warm rag. "Wipe your face, baby. Does your opponent look as bad as you do?"

"Yeah, probably," Rachel said with the hint of a smile.

"If you and Sam fight like this, do you think Mrs. Montgomery will let you keep coming to the barn?" Chad hated to ask that question, especially considering his horse-boarding options were limited.

The stricken look on Rachel's face indicated she hadn't thought that far ahead. "Oh, Daddy! What if I can't ride there anymore? What am I going to do?"

"Let's not borrow trouble." That was something Chad's mom used to say, and frankly, he couldn't believe he was saying it now. "I'll call Mrs. Montgomery in a bit. I'm sure we can work something out."

"Will you really? I know I shouldn't have been fighting. I've never done anything like that before. But Sam made me so mad."

Chad put a hand on his daughter's cheek. "I'll talk to Kelbie. But that doesn't mean you're not in serious trouble. There will be a punishment associated with this." He just had to figure out what it would be. "Tell me why you and Samantha were going at it."

Rachel hesitated so long he was afraid she might not answer. "It was sort of about Mom."

"Your mother?" Why would they be fighting about Lynn? "What about her?"

Rachel sat up. "Sam said Mom left because she couldn't stand being around me. That's not true, is it?"

Chad pulled his daughter into his arms. "Oh, baby, of course not." As far as he was concerned Lynn should be damned to the seventh level of hell. "Your mother was, uh, she was confused. It had nothing to do with you or Hannah." Talk about a half-baked explanation.

What was really going on? And speaking entirely self-ishly, how could he and Kelbie have any kind of relationship when their kids hated each other? Probably not. He knew from experience that a relationship was hard enough to maintain without external forces. Add teenage animosity to the equation and they'd really have a problem.

If he was smart he'd run as far and as fast as he could.

Chapter Fifteen

"Samantha! Samantha Jane Montgomery, you let me in this instant!" Kelbie put her ear to the locked door. She couldn't hear a thing. Damn—she'd have to find the key, which was stashed in the junk drawer.

It took almost thirty minutes before she scored. "Aha!" Kelbie held up the elusive key and stomped to Samantha's room to corner her quarry. Sam was huddled on her bed, face turned to the wall.

"Young lady, roll over and talk to me."

Sam complied. Wow! Streaky mascara, puffy eyes and a red nose—she wouldn't want that picture in the yearbook.

"It wasn't my fault," she declared, before wiping her nose on her sleeve.

"Whose fault was it then?"

"Hers."

"So what did Rachel do that made you so mad?" Kelbie figured she'd probably need a large shaker of salt to believe her daughter's explanation.

"She said Daddy wasn't here because he couldn't stand me."

"Does Rachel know your dad died?" Kelbie was fairly sure there was more to this tiff than she was hearing.

"I don't know."

"What did you say to her?"

Sam didn't answer. Her chatterbox daughter wasn't talking? Definitely suspicious.

"Fess up. I'll get it out of you sooner or later."

"I might have, uh, said something about her mom leaving town to get away from her."

"Samantha!" Kelbie was shocked by her daughter's cruelty. Then it hit her. This fight wasn't about their parents. It all had to do with jealousy.

She took a shot in the dark. "How does Colin fit into this?" Kelbie knew he was only the tip of the iceberg, but she decided to start with the easy one.

"Mother!" Samantha's flushed face told her she'd hit her mark.

"Well?" Kelbie was prepared to sit there until she got the entire story.

"Okay." The teen sighed as though she had the weight of the world on her shoulders. "Colin's been spending all his time with Rachel." Sam sniffed. "He coaches her and he rides with her. He's never done that for me." She flopped back and pulled the pillow over her head.

Kelbie was trying not to smile. When she had sufficiently stifled that urge she lifted the edge of the pillow.

"Why doesn't he pay attention to me?" Sam wailed.

"Could it be because you ride Western and Rachel does hunters, just like he does?" When in doubt go with logic.

"I don't know," Sam groused, but Kelbie could tell she reluctantly agreed.

"And I've heard he has a girlfriend that he met at a Young Riders' competition."

"Yeah, I heard that, too," Sam said with a sigh. "I've been trying to ignore it."

"So fighting about him was kind of silly, wasn't it?"

"Yeah, I guess so," Sam agreed, albeit reluctantly.

"Good. We have that one out of the way. I'm not sure what to do with you. But I can guarantee that you're not going to get off scot-free. You cannot be tussling like some kind of hooligan. For right now stay in your room." Kelbie patted her daughter's leg before she went back to the kitchen.

She was at her wits' end about how to handle this situation. She needed to know what Rachel had told her dad, and second, what he was planning to do about the situation. Kelbie thought it was important for the punishments to be fairly equal. There was no time like the present to ask, so she picked up the phone.

"Hi," she said when Chad answered. "This is Kelbie Montgomery. Do you think we could meet tomorrow for coffee? We need to discuss our daughters."

She wasn't sure how he'd take that suggestion, but she hoped he'd be receptive.

"That's a great idea. The morning is best for me. You tell me when and where. I have to be back at the base by noon. Does that work for you?"

"That's good. Do you know Pearlie May's Coffee Shop?"

"Not really. Is it hard to find?"

"It's on the highway across from the mall. The hot pink building that looks like a 1950s diner. You can't miss it."

"I've seen it. What time?"

"Is ten o'clock okay?"

"I'll be there."

He seemed quite amiable. Hopefully, they could work this out.

PEARLIE MAY'S PARKING LOT was packed with pickups, stock trailers, 18-wheelers and Harleys when Kelbie pulled in. There were a couple of high-dollar German vehicles thrown in for variety.

The aroma that greeted her at the door was as familiar as her mom's kitchen—a fragrant combination of crisp bacon, hot coffee and cinnamon.

"Hey, girl, whatcha doin' here at this time of the day? Cravin' one of my breakfast rolls?" Pearlie May called across the busy restaurant.

Kelbie and she had known each other since the second grade. Pearlie May and her husband, Tom Jenkins, had bought the coffee shop shortly after they were married, and they'd been busting their butts ever since.

"I didn't know you were working today," Kelbie answered.

"Sue Ellen's baby is sick and she had to stay home. So I'm filling in." Pearlie May waved a menu toward a couple of empty booths. "Take a seat and I'll bring you some coffee," she said before strolling off under the admiring gaze of more than a few male patrons. That wasn't surprising—she was statuesque, well-endowed and didn't mind flaunting it.

Kelbie chose a booth in the front window so she could catch Chad as he walked in. This situation was awkward enough without forcing him to wander around looking for her.

There he was, Mr. Sexy. What was it about a guy in a flight suit—that made a girl's libido sit up and whistle Dixie?

She waved to get his attention. "Chad, over here."

He took off his hat and sunglasses and stuffed them in one of his many zippered pockets. "They canceled my noon meeting so I have a little longer than I thought." He scooted in across from her.

Pearlie May sashayed over just as Kelbie had known she would. Married or not, she never failed to check out a hot guy. Not that she'd ever cheat on Tom. They were so lovey it was almost disgusting.

"Would ya' like some coffee, big guy?" Flirting was in Pearlie May's blood.

"Sure." He held up his heavy ceramic mug while she poured.

"Can I interest you in one of my cinnamon rolls? They're famous across Oklahoma."

Although the question was addressed to Chad, Kelbie answered. "I want one, hot with butter."

"Sounds good to me, too," he agreed.

"What did I just order?" he asked after Pearlie May sashayed off.

"A huge pastry swimming in melted butter," Kelbie said with a grin. "It has more calories than a supersize meal deal."

"Oh, okay." Chad stirred cream into his coffee. "I suppose we have to get down to business. What are we going to do about our kids?"

She'd rather try on bathing suits in a communal dressing room than have this conversation, but procrastination never solved a problem. "I'm not sure."

A CASUAL OBSERVER MIGHT assume that two friends were having midmorning coffee. But friendship was the last thing on Chad's mind, especially with this feisty, sexy redhead.

And that was a really bad idea. He'd sworn off women for a reason—namely his girls and his career—and even if he was in the market, Kelbie Montgomery wouldn't be a good candidate. She was as rooted in Wheatland as he was an outsider.

"Here you go, hon." The cinnamon bun Pearlie May placed before him was the size of a large dinner plate, and it was covered in enough melted butter to float a battleship. Holy smoke, Kelbie hadn't been kidding about the calories, not to mention the cholesterol.

"Am I supposed to eat all of this?" Chad felt like a wuss for even asking, especially since Kelbie was attacking hers with the enthusiasm of a starving bear.

"Eat only what you want. No one will impugn your manhood if you don't clean your plate."

Chad took a big bite. "This is good." In fact, it was excellent.

They ate for a few minutes before he put his fork down. "Back to our daughters… I hope you have some insight that I'm missing."

"I just might. Sam's first story was that they got in a fight about their parents, and that it led to some pretty nasty insults. She's blaming Rachel, and I suspect the reverse is true. Is that what you heard, too?"

"Pretty much. Actually, that was all I could get out of Rachel." What else was there?

"Unless I'm mistaken, this is typical teenage trouble, except that it got out of control. What I'm going to tell you is strictly between the two of us."

Chad nodded. "Sure."

"At least on the surface, this is about a boy." She didn't share her suspicious about Sam's insecurities regarding Rachel.

Chad opened his mouth and then immediately closed it. "They were brawling over a guy?"

"That's what I hear. Sam's jealous that Colin is spending so much time with Rachel. And Rachel apparently told her to go stuff herself."

Chad took a deep breath. A boy? Rachel wasn't old enough to be interested in a guy, much less get into a fistfight over him. Was she? He was obviously guilty of a whole lot of wishful thinking.

"Please tell me Rachel isn't dating this Colin character."

He wasn't sure he was going to survive until Rachel went to college.

"Don't worry. Like I told you, he has a girlfriend his age. Sam also has a crush on Colin and it's totally one-sided. He treats most of the girls at the barn like friends or little sisters. I'm sure Rachel is no exception."

That was encouraging. "Where do we go from here?" Chad would take any help he could get.

Kelbie ate another bite of roll before she spoke. "This is just my opinion, but I think we need to make the girls regret deciding to solve their problems by fighting. As for as the true reason for the fight, I suspect this is something they have to settle themselves. If you don't mind, I'd like to coordinate their punishments so that no one gets the short end of the stick."

That sounded good to him. "What do you suggest?"

"I'd like to see them work together, preferably doing something disgusting."

Chad didn't miss the twinkle in her eye. "What do you have in mind?"

"I have a friend who owns a pig farm. He's always looking for people to clean out stalls." Her grin was the devil's own. "Have you ever smelled a pig farm?" she asked innocently.

Chad hooted. "That's brilliant. Rach will absolutely hate it."

"Sam, too," Kelbie agreed. "So, do we have a deal?" She put her hand out, obviously expecting him to shake it. Instead he twined their fingers together.

Chad wasn't quite sure why he'd done that. One minute he was ready to jump into a relationship with both feet and then his common sense would kick in. Kelbie Montgomery would never leave Wheatland, and with his job in the air force, that was a huge problem.

Should he ignore his concerns and hope they went away? Should he act on this attraction regardless of the risks to both of them? Chad was never indecisive, because for a pilot that could be a killer. But in this situation there was nothing to do but wait and see how it all played out.

Chapter Sixteen

Kelbie had forgotten how nice it was to hold hands with an attractive man. It was almost mesmerizing. Then Chad broke the spell.

"Now that we have a game plan for the girls, why don't you tell me about yourself?"

"What…what would you like to know?" Kelbie retrieved her hand and gave him a smile that was as phony as a three-dollar bill. Besides, how was her past at all relevant to anything? "I'm not very interesting. I grew up in Wheatland, graduated from the local high school, went to the University of Oklahoma, got married and became a widow. Now I work for the Chamber. There's not much to tell."

She looked down and realized she was shredding her napkin.

Chad glanced at the destroyed paper and smiled seductively. "I'm sure there's a lot more to you than that. And since we're going to be spending time together, for the sake of our kids, we should get to know each other. I'll give you my bare-bones history and then you can ask me anything you want."

Kelbie picked up another napkin but immediately put it down.

"So here goes," Chad said. "I grew up in Fort Walton Beach in the Florida Panhandle. My folks still live there. And yes, I was a beach bum. It was a hard life but someone had to do it." He laughed. "Then I went to the Air Force Academy and fell in love with flying. And now I'm making my way through the minefield of single parenthood. I told you a bit about my ex but there's more to it. My gut says that Lynn is involved in something more radical than a religion or even finding herself. I'm not sure what it really is." He took a deep breath. "The one thing I do know is that there's no way in hell my daughters are getting anywhere near that B.S." He paused. "Do you know what my worst fear is?"

No, but Kelbie could well imagine.

"That Lynn will come back and want the girls. This time she's not getting them. That would be over my dead body, or someone else's."

It was obvious he wasn't exaggerating. There would be hell to pay if someone tried to take away his kids.

WHY HAD HE LAID IT ALL out like that? If Kelbie had an ounce of sense she'd run out of this place and never look back. Crap, he'd practically threatened to kill someone.

"I understand how you feel," she said with a decisive nod. "If anyone tried to hurt Sam he'd have to come through me." Kelbie glanced at her watch. "Listen, I have a meeting in ten minutes and it's all the way across town, so I have to run. I'm sorry."

Chad knew a cop-out when he saw one. She didn't want to reciprocate by spilling *her* guts. So be it—at least for now.

"But I do have an idea." She picked up her purse. "Why don't you and the girls come to the house Saturday night for dinner? That will give me a chance to make arrangements with the pig farmer, and we can talk to Sam and Rachel about it together."

"That sounds fine." This was one of the few Saturdays he didn't have a work-related social engagement.

"Great." Kelbie jumped up make her getaway. "I'll call you to let you know the time," she said, right before she scooted out the door.

He made her nervous. Good. Turnabout was fair play. She got him hot and bothered, and by all rights that should be enough to send him running for cover. Why he wasn't listening to his basic survival instincts?

Later that night Chad got up the courage to inform Rachel and Hannah about their dinner plans. As he suspected, Hannah was delighted. Not so Rachel.

"You didn't tell her we'd come, did you?" she wailed.

"I certainly did. You and Samantha have to learn to get along. You do plan to keep on riding, don't you?" His question garnered a nod.

"As I see it, the only place to ride and take lessons is at Mrs. Montgomery's barn. Isn't that right?"

Although she was clearly reluctant, Rachel nodded again.

"So, we're going to dinner at their house."

"I'll bet Sam's gonna sh—uh, have a fit when she finds out."

That was a sucker bet. Chad had no doubt that Kelbie was also in the middle of an argument.

THE MONTGOMERY HOMESTEAD was a rambling two-story farmhouse partially hidden behind a screen of mature poplars—the type of landscaping frequently used in the Great Plains as a windbreak.

"I can't believe we have to do this," Rachel muttered

from the backseat before anyone could get out of the truck.

"We've already had this discussion." Over and over and over again. Perseverance should have been that kid's middle name. "I expect you to be on your best behavior."

Rachel snorted. Hannah was being unusually quiet. This was going to be *so* much fun.

"MOMMMM." Only a kid with Sam's flair for the dramatic could draw out that simple word to a wail of anguish.

Kelbie had agonized over the menu and finally decided to do something kid friendly. You couldn't go wrong with grilled burgers, corn on the cob, potato salad and peach cobbler. Sam's job was to butter the corn and wrap it in aluminum foil while Kelbie finished the rest of the meal.

"Do I really have to stay around for this?"

Kelbie shaped the hamburger patty with more vigor than was necessary. "Yes, you do." She slammed the meat on a plate. "And I expect you to act like a grown-up. Look, Sam, the Cassavetes girls are our clients, mine and yours, and as such we treat them with respect."

She wasn't sure any of this was making a dent, but she had to give it a try. They'd had kids leave the barn before; why was it so important for Rachel and Hannah to stay? That was something to think about later. "Do you understand me?"

"Yes, ma'am." The words were right, but the tone of voice left a lot to be desired.

And the evening progressed from there.

Rachel and Sam's contributions to the conversation consisted of a few well-placed snorts and a couple of one-word comments. Chad looked pained, Hannah couldn't stop giggling and Kelbie was ready to kill someone—preferably a fifteen-year-old girl. When the teens thought no one was watching they glared at each other.

"Does anyone want some homemade peach cobbler?" Kelbie asked, hoping dessert would save the situation.

"Can I have ice cream on it?" Hannah asked. "My grandma used to make peach cobbler. My mama wouldn't eat any 'cause she said it made her fat."

Rachel elbowed her sister.

"Well, she did! And stop poking me."

"Girls! That's enough."

"What about you, Chad? Are you up for cobbler with vanilla ice cream?"

"Sure."

"Rachel, would you like some?" Kelbie asked.

"Yes, ma'am."

"Samantha, come and help me in the kitchen."

Her daughter obviously anticipated the drift of the upcoming conversation and meekly followed her out. The minute the door closed Kelbie got in her face, and considering the height difference, that wasn't an easy task.

"Young lady, I expect better of you. If you don't shape up, I'm gonna thump you."

"Yes, ma'am." At least her contrition seemed genuine.

"I love you, but swear to goodness, I don't know what I'm gonna do with you."

Sam hung her head. "I'm sorry, Mom. Sometimes I'm surprised myself. I'll try to be nicer, honest I will."

That was about as good as it was going to get. Just wait until Rachel and Sam discovered they'd been indentured to a pig farm.

"I certainly hope so. Here." Kelbie handed Sam a spoon. "Dish up the cobbler. I'll get the ice cream."

Dessert seemed to relax everyone, at least temporarily, but Kelbie knew it wouldn't last.

"Samantha, Rachel, I'm sure you realize there's going to be a punishment for acting like a couple of redneck wrestlers." She looked to Chad for support. "Right, Colonel?" Kelbie felt that using his rank gave the situation more gravity.

He nodded. "That's right."

"We've decided that you girls are going to spend every afternoon for the next couple of weeks working together at the Parkers' farm."

Samantha knew exactly what that meant. "You can't be talking about the pig farm!" she screeched. "It stinks to high heaven." She turned to Rachel. "Did you hear them? They're making us slop hogs."

Rachel turned to her dad. "Is she *serious?*"

"That's not quite accurate," he said. "What we've arranged is for you and Sam to clean stalls."

The teens stared at each other and then at their respective parents.

Kelbie could feel the hysteria building. "We think that if you work together you'll learn to get along."

Actually, their thought was that the kids would bond through adversity. And Kelbie couldn't imagine anything more adverse—especially for two vain teenage girls—than sloppin' around with a bunch of pigs.

Sam and Rachel were rendered speechless. At least they weren't fighting.

CHAD HAD BEEN DREADING this confrontation, and now that it was almost over he could breathe a sigh of relief. Rachel wasn't happy, but that was too bad.

He was trying to decide what to say when his official

phone rang. They wouldn't be calling him from the base unless it was important.

"I have to take this." Chad retrieved the tiny cell from his pocket. "I'll be right back." He suspected this conversation should be private.

"Cassavetes here," he answered, hoping for the best and preparing for the worst. It turned out to be a bit of each.

The good news was that there hadn't been a crash. The bad news was that the infamous Lt. Gavor had been busted in Oklahoma City for street racing his Porsche 911. It was clearly a case of too much horsepower and too little brain power. Normally a major or a captain would be sent to retrieve the culprit. But considering the implications of the possible involvement of a foreign embassy, Chad had been tapped to make the trip to OK City.

"Kelbie, may I speak to you outside?" Rachel and Sam were doing the dishes. Chad supposed he should be grateful the suds weren't flying.

"Sure." She followed him to the porch.

"I need a favor. I hate to ask and I wouldn't if I had any other choice, but I have to go to Oklahoma City tonight. One of my students got into trouble and I've been asked to pick him up. I called Stacy but they're out of town for the weekend, and Amy Decker's gone, too. I'm not comfortable with the kids staying by themselves. Could they spend the night with you?"

Kelbie swatted him on the arm as if he was her buddy. "Don't be silly. Of course they can."

Chad didn't think of her as a pal. He'd never wanted to kiss any of his buddies, and that was all he could think about when he was around Kelbie Montgomery.

"You do what you need to do," She told him. "I'll take the girls over to pick up their pj's. They'll be fine. I promise."

"I just hope the older girls behave."

"Don't worry. I have their number." Kelbie sounded more confident than he felt. That self-assurance was probably a big act—either that or she was a better single parent than he was. Or maybe it was a bit of both.

Chapter Seventeen

The next afternoon Chad found himself at the operations group commander's house, having a beer and brainstorming what to do about Gavor the Brat.

"What do you think?" Colonel Tim Fletcher was Chad's boss and as down-to-earth as they came.

"I don't know. He's cocky and not willing to listen to authority. In this business that's a dangerous combo. I wish we didn't have to buck the system to get rid of him."

Tim took a mouthful of beer. "If we really want to send him to the Elimination Board the boss said he'll support us. He's as concerned about the situation as we are."

Knowing that he wouldn't have to face the firing squad alone took a weight off Chad's shoulders. "This whole thing is a pain in the ass." He'd been awake most of the night—not that there were many hours left of it once he got back from Oklahoma City—wondering what to do.

"What do you think about putting him on probation this time? If he screws up again we'll let him go, and face the consequences," Chad suggested. "I'm not wild about the idea, but with politics the way they are, maybe we should give it one more try."

Tim grinned. "That sounds like a plan to me. I'm sure

the wing commander will go along with it. I wasn't looking forward to calling headquarters."

Chad could sympathize.

"Now that that's settled, the colonel told me that the four-star general is coming from headquarters for your award ceremony. The head honchos think it's good for the students to understand the importance of your Distinguished Flying Cross."

Chad wasn't sure he wanted a big deal made of what he'd done on that mission. As far as he was concerned it was simply part of his job. "Do you know when the ceremony is going to take place?"

"It should be soon. I'll let you know when it's coordinated with the general's schedule."

"Yes, sir." There wasn't much else to say. When the commander of AETC decided to do something, everyone saluted smartly and said "yes, sir."

BRIGHT AND EARLY Monday morning Chad and Tim were laying down the law to their errant student. Although Colonel Fletcher was the ranking officer, he let Chad do the talking.

"Lieutenant Gavor, you do realize you're in a load of trouble, don't you?" It was clearly a rhetorical question.

"Yes, sir."

Although Gavor seemed contrite, Chad wasn't convinced it was genuine.

"After a lot of consideration we've decided to give you one more chance. If you mess up, you're gone. You got it?"

"Yes, sir."

"For the next month you're restricted to base. I don't want to see you in your car, or hear that you're out drinking or anything else, do you understand?"

"Yes, sir."

"And if you get in trouble again your dad won't be able to save your bacon."

"Nothing will happen. You have my word."

Chad wasn't sure Gavor's word meant a thing. He just prayed they hadn't made a huge mistake.

Later that afternoon he and Kelbie drove Rachel and Samantha to the pig farm to start their punishment. At least the teenagers were being civil to each other, and for that small miracle, Chad said hallelujah.

"Here we are," Kelbie announced when she turned down a gravel road that led to a large complex of steel buildings. The closer they got, the more aromatic the smell became.

"They buy restaurant and grocery store scraps and boil it together to make pig food," she explained.

"Good God, that stinks," Chad muttered. The minute that came out of his mouth he knew it was the absolute worst thing to say.

"Daddy! You aren't really making me stay here, are you?" Rachel's complaint was muffled by the T-shirt over her nose.

He was tempted to bail on this one, and Kelbie looked as if she was having the same thought. Samantha had her face buried in her armpit.

Kelbie stopped in front of the office but didn't cut the engine. Was she considering throwing it in Reverse? Oops, she'd waited too long. A burly man in overalls sauntered out, eliminating their escape option.

When Kelbie rolled the window down the stink increased, and Chad's gag reflex went into hyperdrive.

"Hey, there, Miz Montgomery. How y'all doin'?"

"We're great. How about you, Beano?"

"Can't say I'm hurtin'." He glanced in the backseat. "So these are my new hands, huh?" His grin was almost as big as his girth.

"That's right." Kelbie got out of the truck and Chad followed suit. "This is Lieutenant Colonel Chad Cassavetes. Chad, this is Beano Forsythe. He owns this farm."

"Glad to meet you." Chad shook Beano's hand, resisting the urge to copy his daughter and pull his shirt up over his face.

"Come on, girls. I'll introduce you to *my* girls." Beano laughed at his joke and his belly jiggled.

Rachel and Samantha glanced at each other before they reluctantly followed their new boss to the closest barn. Chad and Kelbie tagged along.

"See them little piglets? Cleaning their stalls will be your job."

Rachel and Samantha had both turned a bit green. Chad wasn't feeling too hot himself.

"See that sow?" Beano waved a beefy hand at a huge animal. "Mary Ann there weighs right on five hundred pounds and she's mighty protective of her young'uns." He pulled out his tin of Copenhagen and put a pinch of tobacco between his cheek and gum. "She also gets a mite testy, so I don't want you girls going in there with her. Ya hear?"

Rachel and Samantha nodded in unison.

"That's Rory there." He indicated a rawboned man wearing matching overalls. "He'll move the little family and then you ladies can do your cleaning. He'll show you what to do."

"Yes, sir. I sho will," Rory said with a wink.

"It's sure good of you to think of us for your 4-H project. Not many kids would be willing to do this kind of work."

Chad glanced at Kelbie. The 4-H? A reluctant grin tugged at the corner of her mouth. God, she was cute.

The girls weren't quite as amused—in fact, both Sam and Rachel sent them a glare that was as toxic as an EPA Superfund site.

Kelbie headed to the truck, motioning for Chad to follow. She didn't have to ask twice. A breath of fresh air would suit him just fine.

"Let's go get some coffee. We may have to go to the drive-in. I'm not sure any restaurant would let us inside." To emphasize her point, Kelbie lifted her lapel and sniffed. "Pearlie May would have a fit if we tried to go to her place. Once we get on the highway let's leave the windows down. Hopefully that will get the smell out of here."

They were in the truck before she said anything else. "I'm not sure we did the right thing."

Chad had to second that one. The smell was beyond disgusting. It had seemed a good idea when they made the decision, but now… Maybe the punishment didn't really fit the crime.

Chapter Eighteen

Life sucked! It sucked, sucked, sucked! Rachel couldn't believe her dad had agreed to this *stupid* idea. She'd report him to Child Protective Services. Then he'd wish he'd never subjected her to this…this humiliation. She pulled up the white mask Rory had handed her right before Mrs. Montgomery and Dad beat feet.

According to Rory, their job was to shovel out the excrement—that wasn't exactly the word the dude used—and then spray the stall with water. She glanced down at her coveralls. They were splattered with said excrement. Gross! She'd never get rid of that smell. The only good thing was that Samantha was miserable, too.

Rachel was about to unload her last shovelful when all of a sudden she was hit by a spray of water. *What the heck? Samantha!*

She whipped around, and sure enough, Sam was pointing a hose at her. That girl was dead meat.

"Oops, I guess I missed." The twinkle in her eye betrayed that silly lie.

Rachel pulled down her mask. "You are in so much trouble." Sam had at least six inches on her, but Rach had a temper, and that was always an equalizer. She grabbed her hose and turned it on her nemesis.

Sam squealed and started running down the aisle between the pig stalls. Never one to back down from a fight, Rachel was well on the way to catching her when the hose was jerked out of her hand.

"Hey, you kids! Knock it off." Rory folded a length of hose to cut off the water. "You're upsetting my sows. March your butts right over to the office. Mr. Forsythe's gonna want to have a chat with you."

Sam held her hands up in a gesture of surrender.

All Rachel could think about was how pissed Daddy was going to be. She honestly didn't want to upset him. Mama leaving had made a muddle of everything. Sure, she hadn't been much of a parent—at least not after she met *that man*—but she was her mother.

That didn't change the fact that Rachel hated everything about Oklahoma—the school, their house, Daddy's job and the place in general. There wasn't a tree in sight. God, she missed the green. The one saving grace was Colin and the riding. And that was only when Sam wasn't at the barn, sticking her nose into things.

But now Rachel had to face the music. Back at her old school she had a reputation for being a Goody Two-shoes. Boy, they should see her now.

SAM WAS SORRY she'd started this tussle. One minute she'd been holding the hose, ready to spray out the stall, and then something evil had come over her. The next thing she knew she was spraying Rachel. Who would've thought that skinny wimp would turn the tables on her?

Mama was gonna be spittin' mad. Sam didn't want to

disappoint her mom. She'd worked so hard to make their lives better, and now Sam was in trouble again.

Considering she'd been a teacher's pet her entire life, this was so out of character. Sometimes she wished she could stop, but who did Rachel Cassavetes think she was, sauntering in with her expensive riding clothes and fancy horse, and taking over Colin's time? And then there was the other thing that bothered Sam even more than Colin coaching Rachel. She'd noticed the way her mom and Colonel Cassavetes looked at each other. If they got together it would completely change everything—and Sam was happy the way they were.

"You ladies," Rory sneered, "stay right here. Beano said he'd be with you shortly. Ain't never heard of someone being fired from a pig farm before."

If Rachel never saw another pig it would be too soon. And, swear to God, she wasn't ever going to eat bacon again. The idea of facing Daddy was terrifying, but she was pretty sure he wouldn't do much more than scowl and look as if she'd disappointed the heck out of him. But Mrs. Montgomery was the wild card. There was no telling what she'd do. After all, she was the one who'd concocted this porcine gig.

Rachel had barely finished that thought when Sam poked her. "What are we going to do?" She looked as uncertain as Rachel felt.

"I don't know," Rachel admitted. "I suspect we're in real trouble this time. We didn't last even an hour. That has to be a record for shortest employment." She giggled nervously. "What do you think your mom will do?"

"I don't even want to think about it. I'm sure it'll be something hideous. What about your dad?"

Rachel shrugged. Their full-time relationship was so new she couldn't say how he'd react.

"Tell you what," Sam said. "Let's call a truce and see if we can get out of this with our hides intact." She held out her hand. "Cease-fire?"

Rachel hesitated, wondering if this was some sort of ploy, but decided to go for it. "Cease-fire. Not that I like you or anything."

"Me, neither," Sam agreed.

CHAD'S CHILI CHEESE DOG and chocolate shake had just arrived when Kelbie's cell phone chirped.

She checked the caller ID and gave him the bad news. "It's Beano."

Chad's stomach dropped. What had the girls done now? "What do you think he wants?"

"Only one way to find out." She punched the talk button and had a short conversation. "They're both fine but he wants us to pick them up ASAP."

"Why?" If everything was hunky-dory why did they have to hurry out to the farm?

Kelbie sighed. "They got into another fight, and Rory doesn't want them disturbing his sows and piglets. Is this ever going to end?"

Now it was Chad's turn to sigh. "What exactly happened?"

"I don't know. All Beano told me was that they were running up and down the barn aisle spraying each other with hoses."

Crap! Literally. His first headache had been courtesy of Lt. Gavor, and now Rachel was acting like a juvenile delinquent.

It wasn't long before Kelbie pulled up beside Beano's office and stomped on the brakes. Then she put her head on the steering wheel and kept it there. Was she crying? Anything but that—he was such a sucker for tears.

"It'll be okay. Honestly." Chad took her hand. What else could he say other than "how about we send the little idiots to boarding school?" That might get a smile out of her.

"I can't believe my daughter is ready to join the WWF." Kelbie accompanied her comment with a sniffle and a hiccup. "Do you have a Kleenex?"

Chad unzipped one of the multiple pockets of his green flight suit and retrieved a tissue. "Use this, it's clean."

Kelbie wiped her eyes, blew her nose and stuffed the tissue in her pocket.

Chad was impressed with the forthright way she dealt with her tears. She went for the gusto, and with her pale skin that meant a red nose and splotchy skin. Even so, she was darn cute.

"Don't worry, we're a team. We can put our heads together and figure out what to do," he assured her. "And we're a lot older and wiser than they are."

Kelbie looked so vulnerable and so kissable. At that moment all he could think about was kissing her senseless— and that desire only partially came from wanting to console her.

IT HAD BEEN A LONG TIME since Kelbie had had a teammate, and God, she'd missed it. When had the body snatchers abducted her sweet daughter and left a shrew behind? And how was she going to get the old Sam back?

Chad was holding her hand, and he was close enough that she could count his long eyelashes. That alone was enough to make her heart stutter, but add in his tantalizing voice and she could almost believe in happy endings.

Nope—not going to happen! She needed to hop out of the truck and get a grip. That sounded like a good plan until Chad pulled her into his arms. At first Kelbie thought he was simply trying to comfort her. Then he lowered his head and had his way with her mouth.

That man knew how to kiss. It was firm but not too hard, soft but definitely not mushy, and it was the most erotic and romantic thing she'd ever experienced. She melted like a Hershey's Kiss on a hot Oklahoma sidewalk.

Chad finally pulled away. "Wow."

"Uh-huh." What else could she say?

He gave her another gentle peck before he released her and sat back. "Let's not do anything drastic until after we've had a chance to talk. Can you go to dinner with me tonight?"

"Uh-huh." Coherent speech was beyond her ability.

The next thing she knew they were in the office, staring down their misbehaving kids.

"Sam, here's how this will work. I'm taking you home and then Colonel Cassavetes and I are going to dinner so we can decide how to proceed." She was using her best take-no-prisoners voice. "Then tomorrow or the next day we'll all sit down and talk."

"Ditto for you, Rachel," Chad said.

"Mom—" Sam started to whine, but Kelbie cut her off.

"Don't say a thing or I'll have to read you your Miranda rights. Get in the truck and keep it shut." Kelbie pantomimed zipping her lips.

The girls glanced at each other and then, playing the martyr card for all it was worth, trudged to the truck.

"If this wasn't so frustrating it would almost be funny," Chad said after the kids were out of earshot.

"I can't argue with that." After her cathartic crying jag, Kelbie was starting to see the humor of the situation—not that she condoned what they'd done.

"Let me call Stacy and make sure she can stay with the kids. You name the place. No drive-throughs, please."

Kelbie thought fast. They needed someplace quiet that had good food. "Have you been to the Circle R Steak House?"

"Is that the restaurant out past the mall?"

"That's the one. Give me two hours." She had a few loose ends to tie up. First, she was going to threaten Sam within an inch of her life if she gave her any guff, and then she needed to get rid of her raccoon eyes and the pig smell.

Chapter Nineteen

Chad was sipping a beer by the time Kelbie got to the steak house. He appeared completely absorbed in his thoughts, giving her time to savor looking at him.

"Hi, Mrs. Montgomery. Would you like a table for one?" the hostess asked. She was the daughter of an old friend.

"Hi, Jane. I'm having dinner with that gentleman over there."

"Lucky you."

"He's not, ah…it's not… Oh, never mind." Kelbie could almost hear Marge telling her not to babble.

Chad's hair was damp, and he'd changed into a pair of chinos and an ice-blue cotton sweater that matched his eyes. He stood when she approached, and pulled out her chair. She loved a man with manners.

It didn't escape Kelbie's notice that a cute little waitress appeared almost before her butt hit the chair. She'd *never* had that kind of service here before.

"May I get you a drink?" Although the server's question was directed to Kelbie, her eyes were locked on Chad.

"This has been a really bad day so I think I'd like a *large* glass of champagne. And tell Pete the bartender not to skimp." Kelbie normally avoided special orders, but tonight she felt she deserved a pick-me-up.

"Sure. And you, sir? Would you like another beer?"

"I'm good."

"I'll be back in a second with your drink." The waitress strolled off.

"I'm sorry I'm late." Kelbie prided herself on being punctual, but it had taken longer than she'd thought to decide what to wear. After a mental debate she'd finally settled on a pair of gabardine pants and her favorite peach sweater. Everyone said it was a great color on her.

Why did that matter? This wasn't a date! Or was it? *No. Yes.* Heavens to Betsy! What was wrong with her?

They made small talk until the waitress plopped a giant iced-tea glass full of champagne on the table. "Pete says to have a ball."

"I guess she took you at your word." Chad indicated Kelbie's drink.

"Looks like."

After they ordered dinner and chatted some more, Kelbie brought up the subject they'd both been avoiding. "What do we do next?"

He leaned back in his chair. "I'll admit I'm at a loss. I was hoping you'd have a magic solution because I'm fresh out of ideas."

"It appears that hard work wasn't the ticket."

"I noticed," Chad said with a grin.

"It worked with my cousin. He 'borrowed' my uncle's car and wrecked it. As his punishment he spent his entire summer putting up fencing around their farm." Kelbie chuckled, remembering her cousin's misery. "You haven't been here in July yet so you don't know how bad it can be."

"I've been in some pretty hot places—Afghanistan, for

instance. When you're in a cockpit and it's a hundred-plus degrees, you feel like you're being boiled alive."

"I never realized that."

"The planes have air conditioners but they don't work properly until you're airborne. But back to the kids... Could we possibly be making too much of this? We haven't heard their side of the story. Perhaps they were only trying to...uh...help each other."

"Yeah, sure," Kelbie said with a knowing grin. "But I will talk to my daughter. I'm determined to get to the bottom of this." She had her suspicions but nothing was certain.

"We've already discussed Colin, but let's expand the jealousy angle," Chad suggested. "Not that I'm any expert on the workings of a girl's mind, but I'm fairly certain that Rachel is jealous of Sam because she's attractive, and she's part of the in group at the high school."

"I've been thinking the same thing except that Sam's intimidated by Rachel because she's sophisticated. Sam feels like a country bumpkin."

"Maybe we're onto something." He couldn't wait until Rachel was out of adolescence. "So what do we do, skip over the punishment and try to get them into each other's heads?"

"How could we accomplish that?"

"What's their biggest passion, Colin excluded?"

"Riding."

Chad could tell the minute Kelbie had her ah-ha moment.

"Are you thinking what I'm thinking?" Her dimpled grin made a glorious appearance.

"I suggest we *encourage* them to coach each other in their own field, and keep Colin out of the picture. I think he's a minor player in this, anyway. Rachel could help Sam with jumping and Sam could teach Rachel some drills."

"What if they argue again?" Kelbie asked.

"Then we go to the nuclear option. No more horses."

"Double wow," Kelbie said. "It might work. I'm sure Marge will help us. She's as tired of their sniping as we are."

About then their food arrived and they segued to eating. No sense in going hungry. The devil was in the details, and unfortunately, it felt as if Satan had been working overtime. But they eventually ironed out a plan.

Considering they were dealing with two girls on hormonal overload, Chad figured it had about a fifty-fifty chance of working. Give him a student pilot any day—one who'd salute and bustle off to do as instructed!

Chad and Kelbie discussed different options before they decided to talk to their daughters individually. There was no sense in opening the door to communal moaning and wailing.

"So we're doing this tomorrow. Should we synchronize our watches?" she joked.

Chad loved seeing her this way. Her eyes were twinkling, her dimples showing and her red hair shining. He'd told himself over and over that he wouldn't give in to temptation, but he couldn't seem to help himself.

"You are so beautiful." Chad was almost as surprised by his admission as Kelbie seemed to be. But that was the truth, and it was time he acknowledged the attraction. It might not be smart, it might even be one-sided, but he couldn't ignore it any longer.

"Uh…uh—" Kelbie stammered. A handsome man had just paid her an incredible compliment. She should be ecstatic, so why was she sounding like a village idiot? Was it because it had been ages since she'd been so flattered? Or was it because she had a bad case of lust?

God, she hoped he wasn't aware of that last part. She wasn't positive *she* even wanted to be in the loop. Add the fact that his smile was almost impossible to resist and Kelbie was afraid she was a goner.

"Thank you, I think."

Chad's grin turned sheepish. "I can't believe I said that. I wasn't planning to, but it's the truth." He took her hand and started tracing circles on her palm. "I don't have a lot of free time, and sometimes it seems like my life's not my own, but I would love to see you more often, without the kids."

Kelbie couldn't resist leaning forward. She felt as though she was being drawn toward him like metal shavings to a magnet. "As in a date?"

He grinned again. "That's what I was thinking."

Merciful heavens! Kelbie hadn't been on a date in so long she was probably as rusty as an abandoned tractor. "I'd like that."

"Me, too. But first I have a huge favor to ask. And this isn't exactly about a date."

"Ask away." Right this minute she'd do just about anything for him, short of robbing a bank. A *date?* How about that?

Chad looked almost embarrassed. "Friday morning I'm getting an award and I'm taking the kids out of school so they can attend the ceremony. I don't know if you were going to be there for the Chamber, but if they could sit with you I'd be grateful." The wink he threw her was sexy and flirty and…wow.

This was getting better and better. "I'll be there for sure, so it's not a problem at all. In fact, I'd be glad to pick them up."

"That's great, really great!"

Then she realized he hadn't told her what kind of award he was getting. "Is it some kind of medal for heroism?"

A deep flush slowly worked its way up Chad's neck. "Something like that."

"Aw, come on. Tell me. I'm going to be there so I'll find out sooner or later."

"Ironically, I'm getting the Distinguished Flying Cross for a mission I flew the day I found out that Lynn had taken off."

That was interesting on several levels, but Kelbie decided to stick to the specifics. They still didn't know each other well enough for her to delve into the touchy subject of his ex-wife.

"Now you've got my attention."

The twinkle in his eye came back. "I was flying the A-10 and we were involved in close air support of a Special Ops team that was trapped in the mountains. The bad guys weren't happy to see us, so they threw some nasty surface-to-air missiles our way. I'm also getting a couple of air medals for other sorties."

The reality of a war half a world away rarely intruded into Kelbie's everyday life. But for a lot of people, having a loved one stationed there was a constant worry. And she knew firsthand how devastating it was to loose a loved one. But she would deal with her private fears later.

"I'm sure Rachel and Hannah are quite proud of their dad."

"I suppose so," he said with a self-effacing chuckle. "But you know kids. Oh, and another thing. The AETC commander is coming from headquarters for the occasion, so that night there's also going to be a dinner at the Wing Commander's house in his honor. Will you be my date to that?" Chad shot her his bad-boy grin. "It won't be all that exciting, but it would be a lot more fun for me if you were there."

That decision was a no-brainer. "I'd love to."

She'd worry about the implications of this "date" with

Chad later. The question was why she was allowing herself to be pulled into his life. Was she willing to have a relationship that could only be temporary? And could she do this and come out unscathed in the end?

The military meant the world to Chad, just as it had to Jason, and that scared her to death.

Chapter Twenty

The remainder of the week was fairly uneventful. Hannah was happy at school—thank goodness. Rachel had agreed, somewhat reluctantly, to tutor Sam in jumping. And if Chad wasn't mistaken, she seemed almost enthusiastic about learning the drill team choreography. In other words, the cease-fire was working, at least for the moment.

Chad hadn't told his daughters about his date with Kelbie, nor had he mentioned that she was taking them to the award ceremony. Hannah would think it was cool. As for Rachel, well, the chances of her clapping her hands in glee were pretty slim.

On Thursday evening, Chad knew the time for reckoning had come. To be perfectly honest, he thought about Kelbie almost every waking minute. It wasn't logical. It wasn't practical. And it was a lot more painful than an adolescent crush, but he couldn't change it. This obsession with Kelbie was a very bad idea, but common sense rarely came into play regarding attraction and desire.

"You guys want a pizza?" he asked his daughters.

"I want pepperoni and nothing green on it," Hannah piped up.

"Me, too," Rachel agreed.

"Okay." Although Chad would've preferred a supreme, he ordered the requested pepperoni. No sense arguing over a pizza when he was about to break the news that he planned to start dating.

When the doorbell rang Rachel was in her room plugged into her iPod and Hannah was running around the back-yard with Piper.

Chad paid the deliveryman and then went to the back door. "Dinner's on!" he yelled. The next stop was Rachel's room. "Pizza's here," he pantomimed. He'd discovered that sometimes that was the only way to communicate.

Once he'd loaded them up on soft drinks and pizza— a kid's ultimate meal—he lobbed the conversational bomb. "Mrs. Montgomery will be taking you to the cere-mony tomorrow."

"Really?" Hannah said.

"Yeah."

"Why?" Rachel asked, narrowing her eyes suspiciously. That wasn't a good sign.

"Because I'll be on the stage and I don't want you to sit by yourselves."

"Why can't we go with Mrs. Decker?" Rachel asked. Of all the times for her to be logical, why did she pick now?

Falling back on a variation of I said so, Chad replied, "Because I've already asked Mrs. Montgomery."

"Okay," Hannah agreed. "Rach and I don't want to sit by ourselves, do we, Rach?"

"I guess not," she admitted reluctantly.

Now was as good a time as any. "I'm also taking Mrs. Montgomery to the dinner at the Wing Commander's house."

Rachel choked on her soft drink. "Why?"

He needed to be honest. "I like her a lot," he answered. He was tired of being careful, and lonely.

"You *have* to be kidding!" Rachel threw down her piece of pizza. "Sam told me you'd been making eyes at her mom and I said she was nuts. But she's right, isn't she?"

"It doesn't matter 'cause we'll be moving soon, won't we, Daddy?" Hannah looked back and forth between her sister and her dad.

"Where did you get that idea?" Chad never ceased to be amazed at what went on in his children's heads.

"Piper said we're military brats and military brats never stay anywhere long."

Chad pulled his baby onto his lap. "Punkin, we're not leaving here, at least not for the next couple of years." Unless he got promoted. Then everything could change.

"Yeah, right." Rachel obviously wasn't convinced. "Personally, I can't wait to get out of here."

Sometimes parenthood sucked.

KELBIE HAD KNOWN Sam wouldn't be happy about her date, but she'd seriously underestimated her daughter's ire.

"You *can't* go out with him!" Sam didn't bother even trying to keep her voice down. "That's disgusting. Why are you doing something so silly?"

"Because I like him and he asked me." There was more to it than that, but Kelbie wasn't about to tell a fifteen-year-old about her lustful thoughts.

"Well, I think it's sickening." Sam chomped into her Oreo as if she were trying to murder it.

"Sam, I respect your opinion, but I *am* going out with Colonel Cassavetes. Marge is coming over to keep you company."

"I don't need a babysitter."

The people who said patience was a virtue had obviously never had kids. "I realize that, but I'll feel better if you're not out here by yourself."

"Whatever." Sam grabbed the bag of cookies and stomped off to her room.

Kelbie hadn't bothered to tell her that she was also accompanying Hannah and Rachel to the award ceremony at the base tomorrow. No need to make her even angrier by admitting to spending time with her nemesis. If Sam somehow found out, too bad.

Chapter Twenty-One

Although Kelbie been going to military functions for years, first as an air force wife and later as the Chamber of Commerce's liaison to the base, she had never attended an award ceremony. The theater was full of people, most of them in uniform.

She'd been so busy worrying about what to wear she'd forgotten to ask Chad about the protocol. Did they have reserved seats, or should they just find a place wherever they could?

"Where do you suppose we should sit?" she asked Rachel.

"I think that guy might be the usher." The teen indicated a lieutenant who was striding up the aisle.

"May I help you, ma'am?"

"These young ladies are Lieutenant Colonel Cassavetes's daughters. Do we have reserved seats?"

"Yes, ma'am. He told me to watch for you. Come with me." The young officer gave her his arm, and Kelbie felt as if she'd stumbled into a wedding.

"Come on, kids, let's go."

The cute lieutenant led them to the front and seated them next to a group of women Kelbie recognized as wives of the commanders. This was more than she'd expected.

But she barely had a chance to wonder what in the world she was doing there when a captain stood at the podium and called the room to attention.

"That's Daddy," Hannah said, pointing at Chad, who was walking across the stage with a group of officers. The general had so many stars on his uniform he could start his own galaxy.

"It certainly is." Kelbie couldn't help noticing how handsome Chad looked.

The master of ceremonies went through the introductions and formalities before the actual award ceremony began. When the citation accompanying Chad's Distinguished Flying Cross was read out, Kelbie was blown away.

The introduction explained the background of the DFC, focusing on how recipients had distinguished themselves in combat by "heroism or extraordinary achievement" while participating in aerial flight. The rest of the citation detailed Chad's sortie in Afghanistan in which he'd saved the lives of seven members of a Special Operations patrol.

He was a hero, pure and simple.

Hannah tugged on Kelbie's sleeve. "Daddy did all that?"

"Looks like." Kelbie glanced at Rachel, who appeared to be transfixed by the proceeding. It must be strange to realize your father was something other than just a dad.

The pin-on ceremony was fairly short. The general's speech, however, took forever. He was so long-winded that Hannah fell asleep, leaning on Kelbie's arm. When he finally finished everyone in the audience popped up as if they'd been shot from a cannon.

"Is it over?" Rachel asked. Hannah grumbled as she rubbed her eyes.

"I think so. Let's go out front and see if we can find your

dad." Kelbie took Hannah's hand and was starting up the aisle when she heard someone call her name.

"Mrs. Montgomery. Rachel. Hannah. Wait for me."

Rachel and Hannah turned to see who was summoning them.

"Hi, Miss Amy." Hannah skipped over to a curly haired woman as if they were best friends.

"Hey, sweetie." The woman patted Hannah's head. "Your dad's in the lobby. Why don't you and Rach go find him? We'll catch up with you."

The woman waited until the kids left before she introduced herself. "I'm Amy Decker. I've seen you around but we haven't formally met. We live next door to Chad." Her eyes twinkled as if she was in on a delicious secret. "I understand you're accompanying him to the dinner tonight."

"That's right," Kelbie said. "Please call me Kelbie."

"Hi, Kelbie. I have to tell you that my husband and I are delighted Chad has found someone here in Wheatland. Swear to goodness, that man's too danged hot not to date."

"We're not…uh, we're not—"

Amy dismissed Kelbie's protest with a wave of her hand. "Oh, please. If it looks like a duck and quacks like a duck, it's a duck. Or in this case, a date."

Amy was right. It *was* a date. But did that have to mean it was something serious? And was that her resolve she heard cracking?

LATER THAT AFTERNOON Kelbie started pawing through her closet, searching for the perfect outfit. An hour and a half later she'd tried on and discarded so many clothes that her bedroom looked like a department-store dressing room.

"Anyone home?" Marge called from the kitchen.

"Back here. You can help me decide what to wear."

Marge was a no-nonsense kind of gal, so her fashion sense wasn't exactly honed, but Kelbie wasn't about to ask Sam for an opinion. She'd end up dressed like a nun.

"What do you think? The green or the red?" Kelbie held up an emerald-green wool dress with a fitted waist, then a silky red number with a cowl neck.

Marge put her finger on her cheek in a classic thinking pose. "Depends on whether you want to get him all hot and bothered or want to bore him to death." Her grin did nothing to silence Kelbie's inner voice—the one that was screaming, "Hot and bothered! Hot and bothered!"

"What do you mean?" Kelbie wasn't being disingenuous. She really didn't know what she wanted.

"Wear the red." Marge didn't wait for a response before she went in search of Samantha.

"Oh, okay." Kelbie looked at the green dress, one she wore to work—and true, it was boring. She decided to go all out—red dress, fancy French twist, jewelry, makeup, the whole enchilada.

CHAD DIDN'T KNOW WHERE this potential relationship with Kelbie was going, if anywhere. Hannah's comment about moving had given him a lot to think about. Finding a woman who'd be willing to relocate would be difficult under the best of circumstances, and Kelbie was so entrenched in her community he couldn't see her ever leaving Wheatland. He was in the middle of this internal dialogue when Kelbie opened her front door, and rational thought flew away.

"You look great!"

Her red dress clung in all the right places and she'd put her hair up in some elaborate twist. She was sparkly, sexy, and so delicious he could feel a tightening in regions that weren't appropriate for a working dinner.

Maybe they could forget the event and head to Oklahoma City—preferably to a restaurant with candles, wine
and soft music. And then—

"You do, too," she said.

Chad was so engrossed in his fantasy about silky dresses
and rumpled sheets that he missed what she was saying.
"I do what?"

"Look good."

"Oh, thanks." He had to get his imagination under control.

"Let me grab my coat." Kelbie rummaged through the
hall closet and pulled out a short black jacket. "This close
to Halloween an evening can be chilly. One minute it feels
like summer and then suddenly we have an ice storm."

If he didn't know better he'd swear she was babbling,
and that meant she was nervous. *Very interesting.*

"I wish I had a car instead of the truck." One look at her
outfit and he'd panicked. His pickup wasn't exactly the
easiest vehicle to get into. "I can help you up, if you'd like."

Kelbie lifted a handful of skirt. "That works for me. Otherwise this will be around my ears."

Chad was distracted by how appealing that would be,
but then his gentlemanly streak kicked in.

"Here." He put his hands on her waist and boosted her
into the cab.

For their second date he vowed to rent or borrow a car.
Damn, he missed his Porsche.

A SMALL DINNER PARTY at the Wing Commander's house
was a new experience for Kelbie, and extra special because
she was with Chad. Although she knew most of the guests,
their reaction to her was different tonight. There were more
than a few double takes when she and Chad walked in together. But even so, it was a comfortable atmosphere.

"Hey, neighbor. That was a nice ceremony." Dale and Amy Decker were the frst to greet them. Dale slapped Chad on the shoulder before turning his attention to Kelbie. "Mrs. Montgomery, I don't know if you remember me. I'm Dale Decker and you've met my wife, Amy. How are things going at the Chamber of Commerce?"

"Of course I remember you. And everything is fine at the Chamber." She'd worked with him on a United Way fund drive a few years ago.

"I'm sorry to say I almost didn't recognize you but Amy saved my bacon," he admitted.

"That's okay. This isn't exactly what I wear to the of-fice." Casual was definitely more her norm.

"Let me tell you, you're looking good." Dale's comment gained him a poke in the ribs from his wife.

Throughout the cocktail reception Chad kept a proprie-tary hand at Kelbie's back. She wasn't sure what to make of it. Was she ready for that type of relationship? The ques-tion had been front and center lately, and she still didn't have an answer.

"Let's go find out where we're sitting. If we're not to-gether we can move the name cards." Chad waggled his eyebrows suggestively. What an adorable man! If she was smart, she'd pull up the drawbridge and guard her heart like a castle under siege.

When they sat down to dinner, Chad was on Kelbie's right and Tim Fletcher on her left. She'd met Chad's boss more than once, but this was the first time she'd had an op-portunity for a real conversation. His wife, Marianne, was a lively woman with a ready smile.

Kelbie's mom had taught her the difference between a finger bowl and a soup mug, and she did know which fork to use. Her problem was she'd never mastered the art of keeping food off her clothes. A red smear was a clear indication she had enjoyed something Italian. A smudge of grease and yep, she'd had a burger for lunch. And so on and so forth.

This time Kelbie was determined to be a lady. She'd nibbled her salad and somehow managed not to squirt tomato juice on anyone. She'd carefully buttered her bread and not dropped it into her lap. And best of all she hadn't dribbled wine on her beautiful silk dress. Everything was going to be A-okay.

"Lobsters!" Marianne Fletcher exclaimed. "I'm impressed."

So was Kelbie, despite the fact that a full lobster—complete with a claw cracker and a bib—was a disaster waiting to happen.

"We're having lobster?" At least with a bib her clothes would be protected. No telling what else might happen.

"Are you allergic to seafood?" Chad had started pulling his crustacean apart, but she was still hesitating.

"No. I'm fine," Kelbie assured him. That was an acceptable social fib. Then she cracked open her lobster's claw and the earth stood still. At least that's how it felt when milky seawater sprayed her in the face and got into her hair. Sheesh, that stuff was sticky. She probably looked like Cameron Diaz in *Something about Mary*.

There was total silence around the dinner table. Kelbie glanced at Chad and noticed that his mouth was hanging open. His expression was so cute she started laughing and couldn't stop. Tears streamed down her face. Mama mia, if she'd been going for sophistication she'd missed the mark! Poor Chad probably thought she'd been raised by wolves.

"Let me help you." He grabbed a napkin and dabbed at her face.

"Let's go to the ladies' room and get you mopped up," Marianne offered with a smile.

Kelbie finally managed to control her giggles and follow Chad's boss's wife to the bathroom. Virginia Johnston, the Wing Commander's wife, was right behind them, chuckling all the way.

These women were incredibly nice. Everything would be fine. And then there was that ultracool guy she'd just left—the one who was trying to keep from laughing, and not having much luck.

Chapter Twenty-Two

It was Sunday morning and Kelbie was shoveling the muck. And that was perfect for her mood. She hadn't heard a peep from Chad. On the drive home Friday he'd gotten a call on his cell and his demeanor had changed. She'd been hankering for a "curl my toes" kiss and he'd left her on her doorstep with a peck on the forehead and a "see you later." In the history of brush-offs, that one was award winning.

The Cassavetes kids hadn't been to the barn since Thursday, which was unusual, especially since the last show of the season was next weekend.

"Hi, Miss Kelbie." That young voice was like manna from heaven.

"Hi, Hannah. I haven't seen you in a couple of days," Kelbie said, leaning on her shovel. Was there a subtle way to ask what her dad was up to?

"Daddy's been real busy with work," Hannah offered.

"He certainly has. I'm sorry I didn't call you yesterday." Kelbie hadn't heard Chad approach.

"Chad," she squeaked.

"Hannah, why don't you go see Patches? I want to talk to Mrs. Montgomery."

"Okay," Hannah agreed before skipping off.

KELBIE, KELBIE, KELBIE. With all that wild red hair pulled back in a ponytail, she looked like one of the teenagers. But she wasn't a kid—no way. He was tempted to kiss her sense-less. Their young chaperones would get a kick out of that.

He spent the last two days in crisis mode, and it had all started with that late-night call. A couple of drunk students had decided it would be fun to try being hood ornaments. Did they honestly think the gate guard wouldn't notice?

Chad had meant to call Kelbie bright and early Saturday morning, but at the time he'd been involved in a high-level powwow concerning the naughty lieutenants. Finally it was Sunday and the young officers had been reprimanded, the general was back in Texas, the Wing Commander was home watching football and Chad was free to head to the barn.

"Hi, cutie." Considering their surroundings, Chad resisted the urge to pull Kelbie into his arms.

"Hi." Her response was curt. Great, he'd screwed up and didn't even know what he'd done.

"When you're through here would you like to go for coffee or breakfast or something?" Oh, man, there were some terrible vibes around here.

"Why would I do that when you can't even bother to phone me?"

Well, he was floored. "I'm sorry. I got waylaid by some base business that I couldn't ignore."

"Well, I guess—" She broke off whatever she'd been about to say. "Why did you pat me on the head like I was some kind of puppy and then dump me at the door?"

"What?" This time he was really flabbergasted.

"You patted me on the head."

Chad couldn't believe what he was hearing. "I did no such thing. And I most certainly didn't dump you at your doorstep."

CHAD WASN'T ACTING LIKE the nefarious dumper Kelbie's overactive imagination had made him out to be. And if she was completely truthful, he hadn't patted her head. But still…

"Why didn't you call me?" And why was she acting like a petulant child?

Chad's sigh seemed to come all the way from his toes. "Can we go over to the bleachers and sit down for a few minutes? We need to talk."

"Okay." Kelbie knew she was overreacting, but her dating skills were sorely lacking.

They finally managed to find a place far enough away from the kids' lessons to be able to talk.

Chad took her hand. "I'm sorry I didn't call you."

"Huh?" He was apologizing—for the third time, no less—so she should say something cute.

"We had an incident with a couple of…shall we say inebriated lieutenants. Actually, they were skunk drunk," Chad said. He gave her an abbreviated version of the hood ornament debacle.

The image was too funny. "Did they honestly think they could get into the base that way?" she asked when she recovered from her bout of giggles.

"I don't know. I suspect it was a simple case of being twenty-two and stupid."

"There is that." Kelbie remembered pulling some dumb stunts when she was that age—not so much anymore. She hadn't done anything remotely scandalous in years.

"Are you still mad at me?"

How could she resist that bone-melting grin?

"No."

"Would you and Sam like to go for pizza with us tonight?"

She'd love to. Sam was iffy. But then again, it wouldn't hurt her daughter to play nice. "Sure, that sounds great."

According to Sam, she and Rachel had called a truce. Although they weren't friends, they weren't hair-pulling enemies anymore.

CATERINA'S PIZZA PARLOR was a fairly typical family restaurant. It was noisy. Kids were arguing. And the parents looked as if they'd rather be enjoying a glass of wine at a five-star restaurant.

"What do you guys want?" Chad asked once they were seated at a table.

Rachel was the first to speak up. "Pepperoni."

"I'd rather have sausage," Sam said.

"No vegetables." That was Hannah's contribution to the conversation.

It was standard operating procedure in the world of parents and kids.

"Why don't we order two large pizzas? One half pepperoni, one half sausage, and then you and I can have whatever we want on ours," Kelbie suggested to Chad.

"Works for me. Okay, what's your pleasure?"

Kelbie knew exactly what she wanted and it wasn't on a pizza menu. "I like everything but pineapple and anchovies. Surprise me."

"I have a lot of surprises up my sleeve," Chad said with a wink.

The double meaning wasn't lost on her. It was hard to concentrate on pizza when something quite a bit more delectable was on her mind.

Dinner was fairly uneventful. Rachel and Sam were almost cordial. Hannah was blissfully oblivious to the undercurrents. And the way Chad kept running his hand along her thigh under the table had Kelbie so worked up she was surprised the entire place didn't burn down.

Where was this relationship going? So far it had been fairly innocent. Was she willing to take it to the next level? The one thing she knew for certain was that she was totally smitten.

After dinner they walked to their trucks. Chad had his arm around Kelbie's waist.

"I'm going to be really busy this week so I won't be at the barn much. I *will* call you, probably every night," he murmured. "And I'll see you next weekend at the show."

He kissed his fingertip and pressed it to her lips. "We can't kiss in front of the kids, at least not yet, so this will have to tide us over." He opened her door and helped her in. "I'll be thinking of you."

Chapter Twenty-Three

Saturday night a cold front roared across the plains in a maelstrom of lightning, thunder and tornado warnings. And Sunday dawned as one of those cold, windy days typical of fall in Oklahoma. The ponies were feeling their oats and the kids weren't much better. Just what Kelbie needed—a bunch of skittish horses and equally fidgety rug rats.

Putting on a horse show involved an incredible amount of work, and this one was no different. Marge was dealing with the flow of the events, parent volunteers were staffing the refreshment stand and Sam was setting up the jumps. It was a family affair and Kelbie was the show mama.

By midafternoon, she was patting herself on the back. The disasters and hysteria had been kept to a minimum, and the kids seemed to be having fun.

Kelbie wandered over to the arena, where the show was in progress. She arrived in time to see a wind-borne plastic bag hit Patches in the face, making him dash for safety in a panic. Hannah was holding on to his mane for dear life. She had dropped her reins and lost her stirrups.

"Daddy!" she screamed.

Chad jumped into the arena and sprinted toward his daughter, but once again he wasn't fast enough.

At the very last minute Patches discovered the gate was closed, so he slammed on the brakes. A stunt rider would have had trouble staying on that bad boy.

Hannah flew off her pony and hit the gate with a re-sounding thud. Her helmet came off in the impact and the child appeared limp as a rag doll.

"Hannah!" Chad screamed as he raced toward his daughter.

Oh God, oh God, oh God. That was the only prayer Kelbie could think of as she vaulted the gate and hurried across the arena. Out of the corner of her eye she noticed another man running toward the scene. It was Doc Watson. He was a vet, but medicine was medicine.

Kelbie fished her cell out of her jeans pocket and made a semihysterical 911 call. Then she spied Paul Taylor also heading in their direction. He was a parent of one of the students, and an emergency medical technician.

"Have you called 911?" he asked.

Kelbie nodded, unable to speak.

"Whatever we do, we can't move her."

Chad was kneeling next to Hannah, murmuring reassuring words.

Sam had caught Patches and walked over, holding his reins. "Is she gonna be okay?"

Kelbie desperately wanted to tell her daughter that Hannah was all right, but what good would that do? "I hope so, but it's way too early to know. Why don't you take Patches's saddle off, rub him down and put him in the trailer?"

Rachel had joined Chad on the ground next to her sister. Her face was so white that Kelbie was afraid she might faint.

"Rachel, Sam needs some help. Go with her, please." Kelbie was trying to forestall a bout of hysteria, but it was apparent the teen didn't want to leave.

"Come on, Rach, let's go." Sam handed her Patches's reins and led her own horse out of the arena.

"Rachel, it would be really helpful if you'd load the horses." Chad stood and put his arms around his oldest child. "Don't worry, Hannah will be just fine."

Kelbie said a quick prayer that he was right. The sound of sirens almost felt like an answer.

"DADDY, WHERE ARE WE GOING?" Hannah's little-girl voice was heart wrenching. "And why do I have this thing on?" She tentatively touched her neck brace.

"We're on our way to the emergency room at the hospital. You're getting to ride in an ambulance. Isn't that cool?"

"I guess." That was a tentative answer.

"Do you remember what happened?" Chad asked.

"Sort of. Not really."

"A plastic bag hit Patches in the face so he got scared and tried to run away. When he found out he couldn't leave the arena, he went one way and you went the other. You hit your head on the gate when you fell off."

Hannah had only been unconscious for about five minutes, but to Chad it had seemed like a lifetime.

Once they reached the hospital, Hannah was thoroughly examined, and other than a minor concussion and a wrenched neck, there was no damage done. Chad, on the other hand, was a mess.

"Listen, punkin, Rachel's in the waiting room with Mrs. Montgomery. I need to let them know how you're doing." He didn't tell her that they'd all been frantic. "Is it okay if I leave you for a few seconds?"

Hannah clutched his hand. "Will you be right back?"

The fact she asked almost broke his heart. Her mother had deserted her, so why would she assume he'd stick around?

"I'll be right back, I promise. The doc said you have to spend the night here, just as a precaution, and I'll be staying with you. But first I need to make sure Rachel has a place to stay."

"Okay." Hannah reluctantly let go of his hand.

When Chad walked into the waiting room Rachel launched herself into his arms. "How is she? Is she gonna be okay?"

Chad smoothed her hair. "She's fine." He glanced over his daughter's shoulder and gave Kelbie a reassuring nod. "Hannah's sore and she has a concussion, but the doc said she'll be as right as rain."

"Seriously?" Rachel looked as relieved as Chad felt.

"I wouldn't kid ya. But I'm going to spend the night here, so if it's okay with Mrs. Montgomery I'd like you to go to her house. Can you do that for me?"

"I guess. Why can't I go home?" she whined. "I'm fifteen. I can stay by myself."

She probably could, but Chad would worry about her all night. "I'd really rather you be with the Montgomerys."

"Oh, all right."

"Thanks, sweetie. Now I need to talk to Mrs. Montgomery." He turned to Kelbie. "I hope that's all right with you." He hadn't given her much of a choice.

"Of course Rachel's welcome. She can help Sam with the horses. There's a lot of work to do after a show. So if you're sure you don't need us, I think we'll go back to the fairgrounds. I left Marge in charge and by now she must be frazzled."

"We're good. Don't worry about us."

"Okay. And, Rachel, you can call your dad anytime you want."

Rachel threw her arms around Chad's neck. "I love you, Daddy."

That was the joy of being a parent.

Chapter Twenty-Four

Kelbie had barn responsibilities she needed to take care of, but the minute the horses were bedded down and her students were all safely at home her thoughts turned to Chad.

Rachel, Sam and Marge were in the kitchen having grilled cheese sandwiches when she came in. "Rachel, would you like to run over to your house and get your dad some fresh clothes? Then we'll take them to the hospital."

Rachel brightened at the suggestion. "Can we really?" Her vulnerability was touching.

"Honestly."

The teen gulped down the rest of her cola and then put her hand over her mouth to suppress a burp. "Right now?"

"As soon as you're finished eating we'll go."

"I'm done." She ran off in search of her coat.

"Marge, if you can stick around, I thought I'd drop Rachel back here and then see if I can get Chad to go out for supper. I'm sure he hasn't had anything to eat all day."

"Take as much time as you like. I feel so sorry for that poor man. He needs a wife." Leave it to Marge to get the last word.

The ride to the base was tense, but considering the circumstances, that wasn't surprisingly. What was surprising was the Cassavetes house.

The decorating genie had apparently made the rounds, sprinkling a little of this and a little of that. The girls' rooms were classic Laura Ashley and the living area was vintage IKEA with a just a hint of Germany. Amazingly, it seemed to work.

"We need to take Teddy." Rachel came out of Hannah's room, carrying an obviously much loved bear. "Daddy says he's losing his stuffing."

No kidding. The poor thing was dribbling polyester guts.

"Do you think he's fixable?" Rachel asked. "Daddy's not too good at that kind of thing."

"Once Hannah gets home from the hospital, I'll see what I can do." Kelbie felt as if she was inextricably being drawn into their lives. What was she going to do when they moved on? And even more important, was she setting herself up for a broken heart? That was a question she'd tuck away for later.

Visiting hours were almost over by the time they located Hannah's private room. Not wanting to disturb anyone, Kelbie peeked in the door before she announced herself. Hannah was sleeping, and poor Chad looked as if he'd had a hard day. His eyes were red, his stubble well past a five o'clock shadow, yet he was sexy as all get-out.

What in the world was wrong with her? The man was sitting with his sick child and Kelbie was thinking about sex—or at the very least lust.

"Hey," she whispered, trying not to wake Hannah.

Chad popped up from the visitor's chair. "Hey, yourself. What are you doing here?"

"I have someone who wants to see you." Kelbie turned to signal Rachel that she could go in.

"Daddy!" The teen ran for her dad. "Are you sure, really, really sure, that Hannah's okay?" She looked at her sister. "She looks so small, and so still."

"She's doing great, I promise. She's just sleeping. Let's step outside so we don't wake her." He escorted his visitors into the hall.

Kelbie pointed to the duffel Rachel had packed. "We brought you some clothes."

"And I brought Teddy." Rachel proudly held up the tattered bear.

"That was a great idea. I'm glad you thought of it." Chad took the stuffed animal. "I'll put it on Hannah's bed." He left to accomplish that errand and returned almost immediately.

"I know you guys want some time together so I'll go to the cafeteria and get a cup of coffee. Call me on my cell when Rachel wants to go home," Kelbie said as she turned to leave.

Chad put his hand on her arm. "You don't have to go. Stay and talk to us. Not that these accommodations are all that comfortable."

Kelbie watched Rachel's reaction before she agreed. She knew better than to horn in on another's territory, and that included fathers and daughters.

For the next thirty minutes they sat in the patient's lounge and discussed the program on the TV—what little of it they saw—and life in general.

"You have school tomorrow, so I think it's time for you guys to go. Did you pack some clothes for yourself while you were home?" Chad asked Rachel.

"Dad." Another one-syllable word was turned into three. Nice to know her kid wasn't the only smart aleck around, Kelbie thought.

Chad smacked his forehead. "Right, you're a responsible grown-up." His comment was made with a smile that only Kelbie noticed.

She was hesitant to broach this next subject, but finally decided to go for it. "You probably haven't had anything to eat since this morning, so would you like to go out for supper? Marge is at my house right now and she's willing to stay with Rachel and Sam. That is, if you feel you can leave Hannah for an hour or so." There, she'd said it and the world hadn't stopped turning. It wasn't as if she'd asked him for a date.

THE THOUGHT OF GETTING OUT of this hospital—even for an hour—was as enticing as winning a couple of Super Bowl tickets. Hannah probably wouldn't wake up, but just in case, he'd leave his cell number at the nurses' station.

"Come to think of it, I *am* starving. Let me tell one of the nurses where I'll be."

"May I go with you guys?" Rachel embellished her request with a "please, please, please."

"Nope, you're going back to Mrs. Montgomery's house so you can get ready for tomorrow."

"Okay." Rachel wisely decided to surrender. She gave her dad a hug and wandered down the hall to wait for Kelbie.

"I don't mind taking her with us."

"No, she'll crash and burn once the excitement dies down. I think she's better off at your house." He grinned. "I'm ready for a big, juicy burger." Or to be more truthful, he was ready to spend a couple of hours with Kelbie. It was amazing how sheer terror could morph into lust when the danger abated.

BY THE TIME THEY ARRIVED at Pearlie May's the crowd was sparse, and that was fine with Chad. He wasn't in the mood for a lot of people.

After they ordered, he asked the question he really needed answered. "Do you think Patches is too much horse for Hannah? He's been spooked twice now, and frankly, I'm not sure I could handle it again."

Kelbie chewed on her bottom lip. "Here's my opinion, for what it's worth. I suspect that back in Virginia he was in a very controlled environment. We're a bit more Wild West out here. What with pickups backfiring and wind blowing, it's a little crazy. Give him time to get used to his environment and I think he'll settle down."

"I'm glad. I was beginning to think we might have to find him another home, and that would have been terrible for all of us." Chad ran his fingers through his hair. "So for now let's think about something else, like food."

He savored every bite of his bacon double cheeseburger. "Thanks for suggesting this. I was about to get grumpy." He rested his arms on the back of the bench. "I'm not much for fasting if I can help it."

Kelbie couldn't have agreed more. "Eating is one of my hobbies."

Chad gave her a look that sent a chill up her spine. "That's hard to believe."

His comment, accompanied by that appreciative once-over, was enough to send her libido into overdrive.

"Speaking of sweets, which we weren't, how would you like a piece of Pearlie May's chocolate cream pie?" It was Kelbie's favorite comfort food.

"Only if you'll share it with me." Chad's smirk gave away what he was contemplating. Or was that wishful thinking on her part? But there was that incident with the banana split. Food and that man were an erotic combo.

"Count me in." Kelbie signaled the waitress and ordered a piece of pie with two forks and two cups of decaf.

Sharing a delectable dessert was only a prelude to what she really wanted. She should feel ashamed. She was contemplating seducing a guy whose daughter was in the hospital.

Kelbie was in the middle of her mental castigation

when she realized something very important. Controlling her growing attraction would be like trying to hold back a tidal wave.

Chad turned his fork over and licked off a dab of whipped cream. "You know something? I'm tired of avoiding this issue." He ate another bite of pie. "I want to take you to bed and cover every inch of your beautiful skin with whipped cream and then lick it off, inch by inch."

"What?" Did he really say that or was she hallucinating? And if she was dreaming, she hoped she wouldn't wake up.

"Sooner or later we *will* make love, and when we do, I plan to spend a very long time making sure we're both happy." Chad's smile was slow and seductive. "I know you have reservations, and I have to admit some of them are valid. I've been arguing with myself, too. But I think I've resolved my concerns and I'm a patient man. I can wait until you're ready."

What could Kelbie say to that?

Talk on the ride to the hospital was minimal, primarily because her ability to carry on a conversation had vanished. Chad had said he wanted to take her to bed, and heaven help her, she really wanted to let him. But was she ready for that kind of commitment?

Kelbie was tempted to drop her passenger off at the front door, but that would only delay the inevitable. Her logical mind told her they needed to discuss his declaration. Her libido smacked her upside the head and screamed "Are you kidding?" Only one of them could win—and hopefully it wasn't her brain. She wanted to kiss him senseless, and then tear off his clothes and have her way with him.

Kelbie found the most deserted corner of the parking lot and hoped that nature would take its course. When she turned off the ignition the inside of the car went dark. The only illumination was cast by a streetlight half a block away. It was a great place for a mugging, or something a bit more…sensual.

"Did I tell you how gorgeous you are?"

She could barely see him, but the way he was leaning over the console told her everything she needed to know. Chad Cassavetes was about to kiss her, and kiss her and kiss her.

This was a life changing moment. They had so many obstacles to overcome in order to have a relationship. She knew from experience how dangerous it was to give her heart to an air force man. But—and this was hard to admit—she'd wanted this almost from the moment she saw him on that deserted highway.

GETTING INVOLVED WITH Kelbie—a girl with roots deep in the Oklahoma soil—was dangerous to his career and everything he ever thought he wanted. But Chad had to admit that he wasn't in control of any of this. It had to be fate, or destiny, or a guardian angel with quite a sense of humor. Whatever it was, he was along for the ride.

Chad hadn't made out in a car since college, and more than likely he'd pay for it with a considerable amount of back pain, but that wasn't about to deter him. A long, hot, wet kiss was exactly what the doctor ordered.

Chapter Twenty-Five

The moment Chad's lips settled on hers a thousand butterflies took up residence in Kelbie's stomach. And when he threaded his fingers through her hair and pulled her close, she had to restrain herself from ripping open his shirt. The kiss quickly grew from a gentle touch of the lips to a sensual, sexy, blow-the-top-of-her-head-off erotic experience.

In a brief moment of clarity—between lust and…more lust—Kelbie told herself that she was *not* getting seriously involved with a pilot. But that was before he reached under her shirt and caressed her aching breasts with his big, warm hands.

CHAD'S MIND WAS IN overdrive, while all his other body parts were on autopilot. He couldn't remember the last time he'd desired someone as much as he craved Kelbie. He wanted to be in her and around her. But that was for another day and place.

The way they were going they could be busted for indecent exposure, and wouldn't the brass love that? So as tempted as Chad was to pull her into his lap and ravage her, he somehow managed to hold on to his sanity.

"Um…I think we should, uh…quit while we can." Was that him making that croaky sound?

"Hmm?"

The fact that Kelbie was kissing his neck presented a big problem. They really needed to cease and desist, but he didn't want to.

"We're in a public parking lot." The windows were so steamed it was almost impossible to see in, and that was a problem in itself.

Steamed windows, parked car. They were asking for trouble.

"Merciful heavens." Kelbie jumped away from him as if she'd been shot. "What was I thinking? Oh jeez, oh jeez. I am so sorry."

Even in the dim light Chad could see that her face was as red as her hair. He wrapped a strand of that liquid fire around his finger. "There's nothing to be sorry about. It was wonderful, and we're going to do it again soon. But for now, I need to go see my little one." Chad kissed Kelbie one last time before he climbed out of the truck and strolled across the parking lot.

RACHEL AND SAM WERE IN bed when Kelbie got home. Marge was watching a chick flick and enjoying a glass of wine.

"Please tell me there's some of that wine left."

"Do you mean this?" Marge held up a half-full bottle.

Kelbie wished she could jerk it out of her friend's hand. She hadn't been this…this…whatever in ages—maybe never.

Good old Marge handed her a glass. "Pray tell, what did you two do?"

Was it that obvious? "I took him to Pearlie May's for a burger."

"That's all?"

When had Marge become a mind reader?

"Not quite." So much for secrets. "We kissed."

Marge smirked as she sipped her wine.

"Okay, we necked, in the truck, in the hospital parking lot." Kelbie said with a huff. "Are you satisfied now?"

"Thank God! I was beginning to think you'd sworn off men forever."

"We only kissed." Kelbie was ready to pull her hair out. This was sexual frustration at its worst.

"Not to worry. I've seen the way he looks at you. It's enough to make *me* hot." Marge pretended to wipe her brow. "As for you, you're as easy to see through as a window. Personal opinion, I think it's great. Now on to a different, but related subject." She topped off her glass.

"I've been considering this situation with Sam and Rachel. They're being civil to each other but they're not friends. And if they're going to be sisters it has to be better than that."

"Marjorie! I only kissed the guy. We're not getting married."

Marge had the annoying ability to tune out anything she didn't want to hear. "I know I'm right."

"Fine, I give. What's your idea?" It was true; she couldn't have a meaningful relationship with Chad when their daughters barely tolerated each other. But this was an obstacle they could perhaps resolve, if they were lucky and devious.

"Here's what I think…" Marge began.

AS FAR AS Kelbie was concerned, Mondays should be banned, and the one she'd just endured was for the record books. Two teenagers, one hair dryer and one bathroom— not good. *Note to self: purchase another hair appliance.*

The minute she got to the office she called Chad's cell.

"If this is the charming Ms. Montgomery, it'll make my day."

In terms of greetings, that was a winner. "It is." Kelbie giggled. Talking on the phone hadn't been this much fun since the eighth grade. "How's Hannah?"

"She wants to go home. I can't blame her. I'd give a month's pay for a shower and a shave."

The thought of hot water running down Chad's naked body was enough to—

"Uh…" It was more of a croak than a word. "I told Rachel to take the bus back to my house this afternoon. I hope you don't mind. I didn't know when you'd get home."

"That's great."

Kelbie could hear hospital sounds in the background. "Marge has an idea about how to get Rachel and Sam on the same page. Would you mind if I don't bring her over until after supper?"

"What's she planning to do, lock 'em in a room together?" he asked somewhat facetiously.

The kids would no doubt think what she had in mind was even worse than that. "Actually, she's planning to take them to the assisted living center where she volunteers, and I'm going with them."

Chad paused. "What for?"

"There are a couple of lessons Marge thinks they need to learn, things like compassion and empathy. She claims they can learn those lessons by working together, and I agree. What do you think?" Kelbie didn't fill him in on the rest of Marge's comments.

"We tried that with the pig farm, remember?" He didn't sound very enthusiastic.

"I know, but let's give Marge a shot. It can't hurt."

Kelbie crossed her fingers. The assisted living folks would definitely not appreciate a teenage brawl.

"I'm sorry. It's been a long couple of days. They won't have access to a fire hose, will they?"

"God, I hope not.

Chapter Twenty-Six

"Mom, where are we going?" It was the second time Sam had asked and she still didn't have an answer. Rachel poked her in the ribs.

Marge cackled, or at least that's what it sounded like. What would you expect? The woman was a retired prison guard.

"We're going out to eat, right?" Sam asked.

"Something like that," Marge answered. Mom was apparently just along for the ride.

"Where?" Sam pressed.

"To a favorite place of mine." Marge glanced back at Rachel. "Do you like cafeteria food?"

"It's okay, I guess."

The twit had obviously never had been to a Luby's Cafeteria, Sam thought. Did they even have country buffets on the East Coast?

SOMETIMES RACHEL FELT like she was stuck in the Twilight Zone. The people around here were totally nuts.

And why was Marge asking about a cafeteria? The one at school was pretty grim. Frankly, Rachel didn't get the fascination about lining up and pointing at food—other than you could get exactly what you wanted.

She liked Marge and Mrs. Montgomery, but the two of them came up with the wackiest ideas.

Rachel decided she'd better get involved in the conversation. "Are we going to Luby's?" Mrs. Montgomery hadn't said a word and that was kind of scary.

"Not exactly," Marge answered, just before she pulled into a circular drive in front of a large redbrick building.

"You've got to be kidding!" Sam exclaimed. "We're not eating here, are we? Mom!"

Mrs. Montgomery just shook her head.

Uh-oh!

Marge pulled into a spot marked Visitor. "Tonight is my night to volunteer and you girls are going to help me. It'll be fun. I promise." She got out of the king cab truck and stood with her hands on her hips.

Sam turned in the seat to look at Rachel. "This is an old folks' home."

"You mean like a nursing home?"

"Yeah. Marge comes here three times a week to do, I don't know, all sorts of things, I guess."

Sam didn't seem sure about much of anything.

"So what are *we* supposed to do?"

Marge opened the back door and answered Rachel's question. "Right now I want you to hop out of the pickup. We're going to find something special for you girls to do. This isn't a nursing home, either. It's an assisted living center and I've already spoken to the director. She said the residents love having young people around. Now, hop to it." She emphasized her command with a loud clap.

Rachel's bad feeling had just expanded into a big, black thundercloud. What if they wanted her to change a bedpan? No way, no how! That was her story and she was sticking to it.

Rachel followed her new commander in chief inside. Wow! This wasn't quite a five-star hotel, but it was close. And the tall, elegant woman in a St. John suit—and yes, Rachel could recognize designer clothing—certainly wasn't the type of person she expected.

"Marjorie, Kelbie, it's great to see you. So these are the young ladies you told me about?"

"That they are," Marge answered. "Girls, this is Susan Harrington, the director of Greenbrier Acres."

Rachel and Sam replied in unison. "Hello, Ms. Harrington."

Why was Mrs. Montgomery going along with this harebrained scheme? Rachel wondered. And even more important, why had her dad agreed to it? This was indentured servitude.

SAM COULDN'T KEEP FROM rolling her eyes—discreetly, of course. She'd been to Greenbrier Acres when her mom had dropped off some baked goods, but this time it was totally different.

Sam didn't know what her mom had up her sleeve, but more than likely it had something to do with Colonel Cassavetes. Those two made goo-goo eyes at each other all the time. Like, duh—they wanted to date and didn't know what to do about her situation with Rachel.

"Come with me, girls." The director started down the hall and then turned to wave them forward. There was no choice but to follow along. "You're running the bingo game. The residents are so excited to have a new person call the numbers." Her grin was downright sly. "Harry Bolivar usually does it but his hearing aid doesn't always work. Plus he gets the numbers mixed up a lot." Mrs. Harrington grinned again. "You wouldn't believe the rumble we had when a couple of ladies both thought they had a bingo. Life's never dull around here."

That was debatable. The only bright spot in this whole mess was that Rachel looked really uncomfortable. That girl was always so put together it was disgusting.

"Who wants to do the calling and who wants to be the rover?" Mom asked. She was obviously channeling her inner cheerleader. Well, she could rah-rah all she wanted, but nothing would make this situation any better.

Sam was trying to decide which job she wanted when Rachel volunteered to rove. Did she know something Sam didn't?

"Goody." Mrs. Harrington clapped her hands together. "Sam, honey, the bingo balls and the microphone are on the table at the front. All you have to do is twist the barrel and the numbers pop up. Go do your thing." She made a shooing motion with her hands.

Sam briefly considered a mutiny, and then looked at her mom's face. Nope, that wouldn't fly.

"Rachel, come with me," Mrs. Harrington said. "I'll introduce you to the folks. Some of them need help in keeping track of the numbers. Cora, here—" she put her hand on a woman's shoulder "—can play ten cards and never lose a beat. Isn't that right?"

"That's for darn sure." In fact, the woman looked like she could wrestle a steer.

"Cora used to own a cattle ranch."

"Yes, ma'am, I shore did," she said, right before she put a wad of skoal in her mouth.

Rachel was trying really hard to keep a poker face. Why hadn't she volunteered for the bingo calling? Because she'd thought roving would be easier, that's why. After meeting Cora, Rachel had a sneaking suspicion this job would require some guts. What if these women got into a gang fight, senior style?

"I'll leave you to it. Don't worry, you'll do beautifully. Marge has said such nice things about you girls." Mrs. Harrington waved before strolling off.

Marge and Mrs. Montgomery had found chairs at the back of the room. Were they plotting new ways to embarrass them? After all, Sam's mom was responsible for the pig farm, and now this.

"Young lady, come here."

Rachel glanced around and saw an old woman who looked like an octogenarian version of Dolly Parton crooking her finger at her.

"Yes, ma'am. May I help you with your cards?" When Rachel got closer she realized the woman's bouffant hair was a wig and her boobs were courtesy of a Wonder Bra.

"Come here," the elderly vamp repeated. "You're a pretty gal. Would you like to learn to dance?" The woman's laugh sounded more like a screech than a chuckle. "I could teach you."

Rachel stepped back. Better safe than sorry. "Uh, gee, that's really nice but I wouldn't want to bother you."

"No bother at all. I used to be a dancer. My stage name was Zinnia LaFleur." The woman had to be at least ninety but she still managed to pop out of her chair and throw her leg up in a pose worthy of the Rockettes.

"Zinnie, dear, you know you're not supposed to do that. You'll hurt yourself. We don't want you to break a hip."

Rachel hadn't realized that Susan Harrington was even in the room.

"Why don't you sit down and concentrate on the numbers." Susan eased Ms. LaFleur back into her chair and pointed at the bingo card. "Samantha just called B-16 and you have one, right there."

"I do, don't I?" Zinnia was so delighted she forgot all about Rachel.

"Let's see who else needs help." Susan waited until they were almost at the next table before she leaned over and whispered, "Zinnia used to be a…what's a polite way of saying this?…a stripper. Now she wants us to install a pole in the rec room so she can learn the new moves. She even ordered a video called *Sexercises*."

Rachel glanced at Mrs. Thompson, unable to tell her if she was actually serious. She had her hand over her mouth, and Rachel could've sworn she was laughing.

"Let's go help Mrs. Harrington?" Susan steered Rachel toward another group of women.

That would have been all right if Mrs. T. had kept her teeth in. But like a good trooper Rachel pressed on with her job. Then she decided it was only fair to share the wealth. She marched to the front table and bumped Sam out of the way. Calling O-64 would be a walk in the park compared to dealing with geriatric strippers and talking about absent gall bladders.

When Zinnia LaFleur called bingo on a B-13 Susan Harrington went into her hand-clapping routine again.

"That's it for bingo. Dinner is about to be served." Her announcement triggered a stampede to the door.

"Thank you very much, girls. Our residents enjoyed having you. They really do like young people."

Sam shot her a glance, and for once Rachel felt as if they were in agreement. This had been kind of fun. Even Zinnia was entertaining. Maybe visiting the assisted living center every once in a while wouldn't be all that bad.

Susan pulled them into a group hug. "Come see us again soon."

"Yes, ma'am, we'll try," Rachel said, and was astonished to realize she meant it.

"Do you think this experiment made any impression on our little termagants?" Kelbie whispered to Marge. "A couple of times they almost looked like they were enjoying themselves."

"That's what I thought. Let's hope we're right."

Kelbie went over and put her arms around both girls. "I'm very proud of you. That wasn't so bad, was it?"

Sam shrugged, but smiled. "It was okay."

"Yeah, it was," Rachel agreed. Then she regaled them with the story of Zinnia LaFleur and her *Sexercises*. By the time she finished Kelbie was laughing so hard her stomach hurt.

They'd almost made it to the lobby when someone called out to them. "Girls, girls, wait up."

The speaker was a well-dressed woman leaning on a walker. She was wearing makeup and jewelry, and appeared to be the most elegant person in the whole facility.

"Yes, ma'am," Sam answered. "What can we do for you?"

"My great-granddaughter is about your age. She used to visit me. But she hasn't come to see me in months. I was wondering if you knew her."

"What's her name?" Sam asked.

"Gina Whitaker. She's such a pretty girl." The woman's smile was sad. "Do you know her?"

Kelbie immediately wished she'd been able to prevent this conversation. Sam had gone so pale her freckles looked as if they'd been drawn on with an eyebrow pencil.

"Yeah, um, her mom is really nice. Why don't you talk

to her?" Sam patted the woman's hand. "We have to run. Remember, talk to your granddaughter."

The minute they were out the door Kelbie put her arm around Sam's shoulder. "Oh, baby, I'm so sorry."

Sam's face crumpled like a used Kleenex. "Gina died in a car wreck last year," she told Rachel. The tears that had started as a dribble were now flowing freely. "She was a good friend of mine and I miss her like crazy. She used to talk about her great-grandma all the time and I thought it was boring. Now I'd give anything just to hear her voice."

HEARING SAM'S STORY MADE Rachel realize a couple of things. First, how blessed she was. Her mom was gone— and she might not ever see her again—but she still had her dad and Hannah. And second, Sam obviously had a soft side she kept well hidden. Losing your best friend had to be horrible.

To tell the truth, Wheatland wasn't all that bad. There were even some things she kind of liked. Sam wasn't exactly a friend, but at least they didn't hate each other anymore. And maybe if they worked at it, they could even be cordial. She wasn't guaranteeing anything, but she was willing to give it a try.

Chapter Twenty-Seven

The next couple of weeks were crazy, and Chad's work was mostly to blame. Not that it kept him from stealing a few kisses in some very interesting venues—in the tack room, behind the tractor, in the hayloft and in the horse trailer.

But back to the work lunacy. He had two lieutenants who were in the middle of a "he said, she said" situation. And yes, it was all about sex that they weren't even supposed to be having.

Right in the middle of that disaster Gavor decided to act up again. The guy had truly unfortunate timing. A farmer out in the middle of nowhere took umbrage that a man in a Porsche was doing doughnuts in his wheat field. Consequently, Gavor had had an up close and personal encounter with the business end of a 12 gauge shotgun.

On the plus side, Rachel and Sam were getting along much better. They were even texting each other.

Hannah didn't have any aftereffects from her accident. In fact, she couldn't wait until the doc gave her the green light to ride. *Fear* might not be in her vocabulary, but it had certainly been added to Chad's.

As for his relationship with Kelbie, things were looking up, sort of—the tryst in the horse trailer had been fabulous.

But with three young chaperones, privacy was scarce, and that was an issue Chad had to solve PDQ. He'd been taking way too many cold showers.

As far as their underlying problem of hometown girl versus move-all-the-time military guy, they were trying to ignore it, at least for now. He was staying put for the foreseeable future, so there was no point borrowing trouble. Besides, Chad was the eternal optimist.

At least he was until his admin assistant stuck his head in his office door and turned his world upside down. His wife was in the lobby and she wanted to talk to him. His *wife! Crap, crap, crap!*

"Are you positive it's my *wife?*" Had Lynn conveniently forgotten all about the divorce and the way she'd abandoned their kids?

"Yes, sir. That's what she says."

Chad huffed out a breath. "Send her in." He *really* didn't need this. Just when he thought his personal life was looking up, Lynn had to come along and smack him on the head with one of her Cole Haan pumps.

It was absolutely essential that he project a cool, calm, professional air. Could he really pull that one off?

"Chad." The voice was right, but the tone was… different. More strident and less cultured.

When he glanced up, he nearly gasped out loud. The last time he'd seen Lynn she'd been a quintessential society mother with tasteful clothes, expensive jewelry and an impeccable pedigree. This person looked more like a South American militant. She'd gone for the full-meal deal— fatigues, combat boots *and* spiked hair. How had she gotten on base without a body search?

"Lynn?"

She plopped in his visitor's chair, elbows planted on her

spread-apart knees, her head on her fists. "Aren't you glad to see me?" It was a cynical question that didn't require an answer. "I want to talk about the kids."

Chad snapped to attention, as if a pole had been rammed up his back. If this fruitcake thought she could waltz in and take his kids, she was crazier than she looked. And frankly, that would be difficult.

"What about the kids?" He couldn't keep the sarcasm out his voice.

Lynn rummaged in the pockets of the old field jacket she wore and pulled out a wad of papers. "I talked to a lawyer and he says I can get custody. All I have to do is show proof of a stable home."

Chad hoped to God he was exuding a confidence he didn't feel. "And how do you plan to do that when no one knows where you are?"

"Central America isn't the moon. Leonard says the girls are welcome to live with us." She spoke the guy's name with a reverence that was usually reserved for God.

"Who the hell is Leonard?" Chad knew perfectly well, but he wanted to hear what Lynn had to say. The second she left he was going to track down the best lawyer in the state.

"Leonard is our leader."

"Leader of what? A cult? A sex orgy? What?"

Lynn jumped up, slammed her hands on the desk and leaned over to get as close to his face as she could. If she'd had a gun Chad would probably have a hole in the middle of his forehead.

"We have a higher calling. We're working for the freedom of the oppressed. We're seeking revenge for the masses!" she screamed. Spittle flew in every direction.

Fan-freakin'-tastic! Lynn wasn't involved with some weirdo religious group. That would be too easy. She was a rabid member of a guerilla organization. It was a wonder the Office of Special Investigations hadn't paid him a visit, or at the very least initiated an update on his security clearance.

But he couldn't worry about that right now. His daughters' safety was his primary concern.

"Let's calm down." Chad took a deep breath, hoping his ex would do the same. But in her present state of mind rational thinking wasn't very likely. She had the wild-eyed look of a fanatic. What in hell had happened to the girl he'd married?

Lynn dropped into the chair. "I want to see my children and don't you dare say I can't!"

Chad hesitated, trying to decide what to do next. "Would you like to come over for dinner tonight?"

"What time?" She stood and buttoned the field jacket over her skinny body. How much weight had she lost?

"Six."

"Okay, but call the front gate and tell them to let me in. I got all kinds of grief this morning. And if you give me any crap, you'll be hearing from my attorney." She lobbed that threat as she stomped out.

The moment she exited the building, Chad dialed the security police commander to inform him that there was a whacko on base, in case she caused any trouble. Then he left messages at both schools to let the girls know he'd pick them up after class.

The fact that Chad didn't trust his ex-wife around their children made his stomach churn. How had things become such a mess?

His next call was to the Wing Commander. "Sir, I have a big problem. May I come by and see you?"

The boss knew all the movers and shakers in town—and if Chad didn't miss his guess he was going to need all the help he could muster.

Chapter Twenty-Eight

Stopping at Braum's Ice Cream Parlor for a hot fudge sundae after school wasn't the norm for the Cassavetes family, and that anomaly wasn't lost on his kids.

"So what are we doing here?" Rachel asked as she dug into her ice cream. "What's going on?"

It wasn't lost on Chad that Hannah was letting her sister do the talking. He took a sip of coffee. His stall tactic wasn't fooling anyone, especially not the girls.

"Your mother is in town and she wants to see you." There, he'd said it and the sun was still shining.

Hannah paused with her spoon halfway to her mouth. The poor kid looked as if she'd just spied Bigfoot. Chad didn't have a clue what she was thinking. Her sister was much easier to read.

"What does *she* want?" Rachel spat the words out. "She thinks she can dump us and then march back in like nothing happened?" She threw her spoon on the table. "Mom probably expects us to treat her like we care. Well, she can just forget about it."

"She's your mother and I think you should see her." Chad couldn't make himself say that she loved them. At this point he wasn't sure Lynn was even capable of love.

But bad-mouthing his ex would be counterproductive for everyone involved. "I've invited her to dinner and I'm asking you girls to be cordial."

Hannah came around the table, climbed in his lap and put her head on his chest. Chad patted her back, vowing to move heaven and earth to keep his babies safe. Rachel's eyes filled with tears and when Chad held out an arm she joined the family hug.

"What do you think we should have for dinner?" he asked.

"Worms," Hannah mumbled around the thumb she'd stuck in her mouth. She hadn't done that since she was a toddler.

"What about Kentucky Fried Chicken?" Chad and the girls loved KFC, but Lynn thought fast food was too gauche for words—and that went double for the colonel's finest.

Rachel and Hannah looked at each other and giggled.

"Let's get a bucket of drumsticks and mashed potatoes with gravy!" Hannah suggested. Their mom hated drumsticks, and as for store-bought gravy, she wasn't a fan.

"KFC it is. We'll run by and pick it up on our way home. Then we can nuke it."

Hannah giggled again and Rachel rolled her eyes.

Chad was the adult in this situation, and he supposed he should know better, but sometimes a man needed to indulge his inner child.

He was desperate to talk to Kelbie. In this world of madness she was his sanctuary.

THE FRONT GATE BUZZED just before six to let Chad know that Lynn was on her way. "You mom will be here in a minute," he announced.

"Great." Rachel bounced her soccer ball over and over. She wasn't the only jittery one. Hannah was running around like a gerbil on speed.

Chad couldn't blame the kids—he was nervous himself. When the doorbell rang, he reacted with equal amounts of dread and anticipation.

"Lynn, come in." He sounded cordial and controlled. Score one for the good guys.

"Mother?" Rachel's expression bordered on horror. "What happened to you?"

Chad suspected she was referring to the combat boots and field jacket rather than asking where Lynn had been for the past six months.

"Is that any way to speak to your mother?" Lynn assumed the imperious tone of voice he remembered from the latter days of his marriage. "Girls, come here and give me a hug."

It was obvious that Hannah was torn, but Lynn was still her mother. She approached step by step, careful not to get close enough for a hug. Rachel simply ignored her. Ironically, Lynn seemed to be the only person who didn't realize there was a five-hundred-pound gorilla in the room.

"Are you going to offer me something to drink?" she asked as she made herself at home. "Where did you get this sofa?" Now Lynn was impugning his taste in furniture. That was rich, considering she was dressed like Fidel Castro in drag.

Chad was trying to come up with a pithy answer when Rachel jumped in. "Goodwill. We shop there a lot." Lynn felt the same way about thrift shops that she did fast food.

"Oh." She moved closer to the edge of the couch.

What was wrong with this woman? She was living in a compound that may or may not have running water and toilets, and she didn't want to sit on a secondhand couch?

Chad wondered if there was something physiological going on, like a brain tumor or a chemical psychosis. If that was the case, he couldn't help but feel sorry for Lynn. But if she was just mean, then the devil could take her.

"Hannah, would you please set the table?" For a change he didn't have to ask twice. Rachel even went out to help her.

"WOULD YOU LIKE A GLASS of wine?" Chad had made a special trip to the liquor store to buy Lynn's favorite.

"That would be wonderful." Her garden-party manners had returned with a vengeance. It was a stark contrast to her appearance.

Chad poured the wine, careful to avoid looking at his daughters. He could picture Rachel's eye roll, and damned if he wasn't tempted to indulge in a little of that himself.

According to the clock, dinner was short. In terms of misery, however, it seemed interminable. The conversation was stilted, the food was unappetizing and the kids were abnormally quiet. Rachel spent most of the meal sulking, while Hannah cowered.

Fun was had by all.

Lynn might not have enjoyed her food, but she certainly consumed more than her share of merlot.

"Don't take this wrong, but would you like me to drive you back to your hotel?" Chad asked at last. "I can have someone deliver your car in the morning." He wasn't about to send her out with most of a bottle of wine in her system.

"That would be lovely." Considering her tone, Chad half expected her to take off her field jacket to reveal a tasteful suit and pearls.

"Come and give your mother a hug," Lynn commanded, apparently oblivious to the fact that the girls hadn't wanted to touch her earlier.

Although Rachel and Hannah did as instructed this time, they didn't linger. Why hadn't he noticed Lynn's lack of maternal warmth before? And should he have done something ages ago to amend their custody agreement? Guilt would gnaw him to death if he let it. There wasn't anything he could do about past mistakes, but he could about the future.

He wouldn't have thought it was possible, but the drive to the hotel was even more uncomfortable than dinner. Chad was desperate for this fiasco to be over, but there was a bigger issue at hand and it was one he couldn't shirk.

"Tomorrow we need to get together and discuss why you're really here."

Lynn opened the car door before responding. "You can't intimidate me. I'm here for a reason and yes, I do think we should meet tomorrow. You tell me the time and place."

"Why don't we meet at the coffee shop in the lobby at ten o'clock?"

"I'll be there, and I'll have Leonard with me." She got out of the truck and slammed the door.

That wasn't exactly a "thanks for the dinner, it was so nice to see you." Good old Lynn. She always had to have the last word.

Chapter Twenty-Nine

The first thing Chad did when he got home was to phone Hank Salisbury, a highly recommended family attorney. Lawyers didn't come cheap, but Chad was prepared to sell everything he owned if it meant keeping his kids.

"What do you think she's after?" Hank asked when Chad had explained the situation.

"I don't know. Whatever it is, I don't think it's good. I can't imagine her truly wanting the girls." He sighed. "You should see her. She went from Sorority Sue to Guerilla Gertie in less than six months."

"Where are you meeting tomorrow?"

"The Holiday Inn coffee shop at ten o'clock. What do you have in mind?"

"I'm going to my ranch tonight. But I can meet you in the morning to strategize. I might decide to hang around and have another cup of coffee, just to check things out, ya know?" The lawyer chuckled.

He sounded like Chad's kind of guy—an interesting combo of good old boy and corporate shark. Now all Chad had to do was ask for a couple days' leave. Considering the maelstrom his personal life had become, and the amount of leave he'd already requested this year, he'd be surprised if the Wing Commander didn't change his status to squadron gofer.

CHAD WAITED NERVOUSLY in the hotel lobby for his lawyer. He was well on his way to a caffeine high—from too much coffee, too little food and too much anxiety.

He'd started his third cup of the morning when he noticed a guy strolling in his direction. Was this the "best of the West" hotshot attorney? With his faded jeans, scuffed boots and five-o'clock shadow he looked like a cross between a bull rider and a roughneck.

"You must be Chad Cassavetes." The man stuck out his hand. Despite his clothing he exuded power. "I'm sorry about my appearance. I had an emergency at the ranch and I never made it back to town last night. I hope I don't smell like a horse."

Chad stood and shook the lawyer's hand. "I'm glad to meet you. We have horses, too, so I'm used to that smell," he said. That had certainly been true in the past couple of months. "I hope you can help me. I'm pretty desperate here."

Hank's laugh came straight from his belly. "That's why people hire me. And not to brag, but I'm damn good at what I do."

For the next forty-five minutes the men discussed all possible configurations of the situation. Chad thought he finally had a handle on it. That is, until Lynn walked in accompanied by Mr. Smarmy, the twenty-first-century version of a snake-oil salesman. He was just as his ex-father-in-law had described him all those months ago.

"Oh, crap," Chad muttered.

"You got that right. I originally thought I'd head on home, but I think I've changed my mind," Hank said. "I suspect you're going to need me here. Do me a favor and don't mention that I'm your lawyer, at least not at first. I have a feeling we'll get more out of him if he thinks I'm your buddy."

Chad was surprised that Hank wasn't wearing suspenders to snap.

It took less than five minutes for them to realize that Leonard— who never gave his last name—was a control freak who was after money.

"Let me get this straight," Chad said. "You're telling me that some lawyer claims Lynn has a strong case to regain custody of *my* girls?"

"That's right," Leonard agreed.

"And you're also saying that Lynn would consider dropping this idea if I could come up with a *bribe?*" Chad was tempted to beat the crap out of the guy. Fortunately, he was held in check by a kick in the shin delivered by his attorney.

"I wouldn't exactly put it like that," Mr. Sleaze said. "Right, Lynn love? You miss your daughters, don't you?"

She was nodding like a bobblehead doll. The way he manipulated her was mind-blowing.

"We'd like the girls to live with us, but if you insist on keeping them here, Lynn would be bereft. In that case I'd think you'd want to, uh, provide her with some sort of compensation. But if you're not feeling generous, we'll be forced to take action. And you never know what might happen in the court system."

Chad wondered what kind of sentence he'd get for breaking the guy's arm.

"Maybe it's time for me to introduce myself properly. I'm Lieutenant Colonel Cassavetes's lawyer." Hank's smirk was pure evil. "I think I should tell you that blackmail is a felony in this state, punishable by ten to twenty years in the pen." His grin got even wider.

"But—but I'm not—"

"Oh, I think you are. And let me also tell you that as an officer of the court I'm honor bound to report this conversation to the authorities." Hank leaned forward. "I wouldn't suggest you try this again, but if you do, make sure you know who's sitting in. I would also recommend that you grab your things and get the heck out of here." He propped one booted foot on his knee, a deceptively casual pose. "Here in Oklahoma us good old boys have a sayin'. Want to know what it is?" Hank drawled, not missing a beat before he continued. "'Don't let the screen door hit your ass on the way out.' Got it?"

Leonard looked as if he was about to have a stroke, but Lynn hadn't said a word. "Lynn, get your bag," he barked. "She scooted off like a robot to comply. You haven't heard the last of us," he said to the men. Although his words were confident, his tone gave away his fear.

"Oh, I think we have," Hank countered. "If I ever hear about you coming back to our county, I'll sic the sheriff on you." He cocked his head. "Did I tell you he's my brother-in-law?"

Leonard jumped up and stomped out the door.

"I think I'll go have a chat with him," Chad said.

"I suspect that's a good idea. Just don't do anything that I'll have to report to my bro-in-law."

Chad followed Leonard to the parking lot. The dolt didn't even notice, and considering his criminal tendencies, that was stupid.

"Wait up." Chad didn't have to yell—he was only a few steps behind his prey.

When Leonard whirled around, Chad realized he had him. The bully was scared to death.

Chad was itching to slam Mr. Slick up against the car, but managed to keep his hands to himself. He did, however, invade Leonard's personal space.

"Stay away from my daughters. You got it?"

Leonard gaped.

"Say it!" Chad demanded.

"I won't come back to Oklahoma. Is that enough for you?" He was making a feeble effort to redeem his macho pride.

Chad moved closer. "As for Lynn, I can't make her stay in the States, but if I hear anything about you mistreating her, or if anything at all happens to her, you'll live to regret it. Do I make myself perfectly clear? Nod if you understand." Chad towered over the skinny wimp.

Leonard nodded.

"I want you to take her back to Virginia, at least long enough to see her parents and get a thorough medical evaluation." He grabbed Leonard's lapels. "I just want to make sure we're both on the same page. Another nod and you're free to go. But don't disappoint me. I have friends who make periodic trips to your jungle and they'd be happy to visit you. They can slip in and out without making a sound. And the things they can do with a knife…"

Chad was doing a bang-up job of imitating Chuck Norris. He couldn't let this snake take Lynn back to Central America without having her checked out by a doctor. And he wouldn't let anyone threaten his kids.

Poor Leonard looked as if he was about to hurl. Dollars to doughnuts, they'd be on a plane to Virginia before the day was through.

"Lynn, hurry up. We're out of here!" he yelled.

Chad stepped back and watched his ex-wife scurry across

the parking lot. What had he seen in her? And what had happened to change her so much? He'd probably never know.

What Chad did know was that life was too short to waffle. It was either quit seeing Kelbie or make a solid commitment. There were too many things out of his control to walk away from something that could be this good. The peripheral issue of their kids was improving. Rachel and Sam weren't best buddies but they were taking baby steps in the right direction. His primary problem was how could they overcome the issue of his career versus her desire to stay in Wheatland?

This episode with Lynn made Chad realize he loved everything about Kelbie—her intellect, her wit, her love for her family and friends, and of course, her smokin' body—not that he'd seen all that much of it. And that was something he had to rectify, right after he laid his heart at her feet.

Chapter Thirty

After his showdown at the Holiday Inn, Chad headed straight to Kelbie's office. He was desperate to see her.

"Hi, Sherry. Is Kelbie here?" He tried to sound casual, but that wasn't easy, especially with his stomach doing the cha-cha.

"Hi, Colonel Cassavetes. Is she expecting you?"

"No, but I'm sure she'll see me." It wasn't macho to sound needy, but that's exactly how he felt.

Sherry nodded and flipped on an ancient intercom. "Kelbie, you have a visitor. Get your rear end out here ASAP."

"Don't yell, I'm coming."

"She hates when I do that," Sherry said with a wide smile. "Here she is."

"Chad! What are you doing here?"

"I had a confrontation with Lynn and her sleazy friend this morning."

"I'm so sorry." Kelbie grabbed his hand. "Come back to my office. I'll get you a cup of coffee."

SHERRY MADE A PRETENSE of going to the printer, but Kelbie knew better. That girl was the nosiest chick on the planet.

"I think I hear the phone ringing. You should go answer

it," Kelbie said right before she closed the office door in her friend's face.

"Chad, why don't you sit down?" She indicated an antique settee.

"Are you sure it's safe?" he asked as he eyed the rickety piece.

"Probably not," she admitted. "I'd hate for you to land on your tush. Here, try this." She pulled a sturdy office chair out of the corner. "Let me get our coffee. I won't be long."

Kelbie sprinted to the communal kitchen. Her curiosity was killing her. What had happened at that meeting?

"Are you okay? And how's he doing?" Sherry was standing by the coffeepot, the Chamber's version of a water cooler.

"I'm fine, but I'm not sure about Chad. We haven't had a chance to talk yet. Hold my calls. I'll let you know when I'm available." Kelbie made it back to her office in record time.

"Here you go." She handed him a mug of steaming coffee. He looked as if what he could really use was a big slug of Jack Daniel's.

"Thanks." He took a sip and Kelbie followed suit.

"Do you want to tell me about it?" She pulled her chair around so they were facing each other.

"Lynn was trying to blackmail me." Chad massaged his temples.

"Blackmail you!" He was Mr. Squeaky-Clean. How could anyone blackmail him? "What about?"

Chad's sigh was long and deep. "Here's the Cliffs Notes' version. Lynn and that sleazebag friend of hers threatened to sue me for custody of the kids. They said they were going to take them to a compound in Central America where they're involved in some kind of hinky revolution thing." He paused. "The good news is that I sicced Hank Salisbury on them."

"You hired Hank?" Kelbie had known Hank since they were kids. He was one of the best attorneys in the state.

"I did."

"Good choice." She wanted to comfort him, but deep down she was hankering for something much more intimate. Was this lust, love or a result of extended celibacy?

"After Hank threatened Leonard within an inch of his life, I took it one step further and cornered him in the parking lot. I'm pretty sure I scared the crap out of him."

"You beat him up?" Kelbie wouldn't have thought Chad would do that, but he might if someone threatened his kids.

"No, not that bad." Chad grinned again. "I told him if he ever tried to take my kids away again I'd have some of my covert ops buddies track him down in the forest."

"Do you have covert ops buddies?" Kelbie asked, not quite sure she really wanted to hear the answer.

"No," Chad admitted with a chuckle. "I was totally bluffing. I also told him he had to get Lynn back to Virginia for a medical evaluation. Her parents are going to have a fit when they see her."

"Do you honestly think she's sick?"

"I do. She's done a one-eighty in her personality, appearance and just about everything else." Chad shrugged. "I don't think that happens unless there's something seriously wrong, physiologically speaking. I'm not positive I would've even recognized her."

Kelbie loved this guy! Give him a psychotic ex-wife and he worried about getting her help.

None of this jibed with Kelbie's life plan, but obviously love had its own agenda. Add in the fact that Sam and Rachel were starting to get along, and she had the sinking feeling she was in serious toruble.

Were their problems solvable? Her life was in Wheatland. She had friends, family and a farm she couldn't leave—or could she? Chad's assignment at Perry was only a small part of his career. If this relationship was to move to the next level she'd face the difficult decision of whether to go with him when he was transferred, or to stay in Wheatland alone. Then there was his job itself. She knew the chances of him being killed were slim, but phobias weren't necessarily reasonable. She still wasn't sure she could risk losing another man she loved.

Now she was being a dunce. They'd shared only a couple of kisses and she was already picking out bed linens. Kelbie shook off that thought, at least for the moment.

"You did what you had to do to protect your kids. You were just being a good dad. I think your white lie was funny, and even better, it was effective."

THE TIME LINE OF what happened next was a little fuzzy, not that it really mattered. All Chad cared about was that Kelbie was in his lap and he was kissing her as if he'd never stop. It was a slow, hot mating of tongues and lips that magically took on a life of its own.

Chad leaned back, breathing hard. "I've wanted you for weeks. I can't tell you the fantasies I've had." He nuzzled the valley between her breasts. "I want to kiss every inch of you. I want to see you blush when I taste you. But mostly I want to see you climax."

Kelbie's cheeks turned a delightful pink. She was embarrassed, and that was even more alluring.

WITHOUT ANOTHER WORD, Chad slipped open the first button of her blouse. Then the second, then the third. It was so erotic that Kelbie thought her heart might stop beating. Chad's breath was warm on the delicate skin between her breasts as his hand inched slowly under her skirt, leaving a trail of goose bumps in its wake.

There, right there. Oh, yes! Kelbie pushed up her skirt and straddled his lap, seeking gratification. She'd never in a million years suspected that making love in an office chair could be so—

"Kelbie, I need you out here." Why was Sherry's tinny voice intruding on her fantasy? She popped up like a jack-in-the-box. They were getting it on in her office. Her office! Where anyone and everyone felt free to walk right in. What was she thinking? Obviously nothing. She'd lost her freakin' mind.

"I am so sorry. *So* sorry." Kelbie tried to button her blouse, but unfortunately she didn't get very far.

Chad moved her hands aside. "Let me do that." He gave her one of those grins that made her weak in the knees. "Lately, I've learned a few things about dressing girls."

"Stay here. Don't move a muscle. I have to see what Sherry wants and then we need to talk." She ran a hand through her hair. There wasn't a darned thing she could do about her swollen lips or her blush. And knowing Sherry as she did, Kelbie was never going to hear the end of this.

Sherry's "emergency" was something minor that she could easily have handled on her own. However, in a way, Kelbie felt relieved. Someone could have walked in on them. They'd dodged a huge bullet there.

"Sherry makes a crisis out of every little thing," Kelbie said when she returned and sat down behind her desk, putting a barrier between her and temptation. Not that it helped much. The Great Wall of China wouldn't be big enough to keep that enticement at bay. She loved Chad, heart and soul, and now she had to find out if that was mutual.

"So?" He looked way too casual with one ankle crossed over a knee.

"So, I think we should go to a hotel," she announced, trying to seem more sure of herself than she was.

"Oh." He paused for a second before he broke into the brightest smile she'd ever seen. "That sounds like a plan."

"When?"

"Right now."

"That's *definitely* a good idea." Although she wouldn't have thought it possible, Chad's smile got even brighter. He looked like a kid with a free pass to a toy shop.

Chapter Thirty-One

Privacy in a small town was hard to come by, and considering Kelbie's position in the community...well, getting together for a tryst wasn't easy. The logistics of trying to be spontaneous were making it feel less spur-of-the-moment and more...whatever.

Kelbie was tempted to call it off. "I feel like a teenager doing something naughty."

"How naughty?"

"Do you think we should do this?" She wanted him to say yes. That would go a long way toward calming her nerves.

"Absolutely," Chad said as he pressed down on the accelerator.

As the highway markers whizzed by, and they got closer and closer to Oklahoma City, Kelbie decided it was time to come clean. She was about to get very intimate with this man, so he might as well hear it all.

"You may have noticed I've been trying to keep my distance from you. There's a reason, and I think you deserve to know."

Chad glanced at her. For a change his expression was totally neutral.

"I told you my husband died in a plane crash. What I

didn't tell you was that I saw the smoke from our house on base. I knew exactly what it meant. So I took Sam to my neighbor's house and raced down to the flight line. All I could see was the fire. It was this hideous ball of flames that reached to the sky, and I knew Jason was in the middle of it." Kelbie took a deep breath. "And when it was over there was nothing left. Nothing but his dog tags. I'm not sure I can do that again." Tears were running down her cheeks.

Chad pulled the truck to the shoulder and held her hands in his. "Oh, honey. I can't promise you that nothing will happen to me. We could be hit by a semi while we're sitting here by the side of the road. Life doesn't come with any guarantees."

"I know. It's just that I'm so scared. I do love you. And even *that* scares me, considering the short time we've known each other." Her laugh was shaky but she supposed it was better than a sob.

"Since we're into true confessions, I should tell you that I've been having some doubts myself. I wasn't sure I could get involved with someone who wasn't enthusiastic about my military career. But I realized that being committed to each other is what's important. We'll work the other stuff out if we love each other, and I *do* love you. This isn't a fling for me, and I don't believe it is for you, either. Am I right?"

"How did you get so smart?" This relationship wasn't going to be easy, and there weren't any assurances that it would last, but they had to try. Still, Kelbie wasn't sure she wanted to go to the motel.

Then came the time of reckoning. Chad went inside the motel to register while she stayed in the truck, getting cold feet.

He returned shortly and held up a key. "We're all set."

He sounded almost as enthusiastic as she felt, and that wasn't encouraging.

"I, uh, I don't know if I can do this," she admitted. Yes, she was an adult, and as such she could do anything she liked as long as it wasn't immoral or illegal. But somehow, this wasn't what she wanted for their first time together. Checking in to a motel in the middle of the day felt…cheap.

Chad slumped in the seat. "I know. Do you have any other ideas?" He was the picture of frustration as he ran his fingers through his hair.

"Let's take a chance and go back to my house," Kelbie suggested. "We can push the dresser in front of the bedroom door if we have to."

He raised her hand to his lips and kissed her palm. "You're a very special lady, you know that?" He didn't wait for an answer before he hopped out to return the key. Then he threw the truck in gear and shot out of the parking lot.

THE HORSES WERE GRAZING in the pasture, the barn was quiet and all was well at the Montgomery homestead. And if Kelbie had anything to say about it, she was definitely going to have her way with a certain top gun dad.

What their first time lacked in finesse it made up for in intensity. Their coupling started as a frenzied mating against the door of her bedroom. Chad pulled at her clothes; she ripped at his. Buttons popped, shoes went sailing and inhibitions flew out the window. Before you could say safe sex—although he was prepared—they were making love on her antique Aubusson rug. Kelbie was pretty sure she'd died and gone straight to heaven.

Even before she climaxed, she knew she'd come home. She belonged in this man's arms and she'd make whatever accommodations she had to in order to be with him.

"If you'll give me a second to recuperate, I'm up for a replay. How about you?" Chad's sexy voice was sexy and lazy enough to drive her wild. The fact that he was suckling on her nipples didn't hurt, either.

"Oh, yes." For round two she wanted a man with a slow hand and an easy touch. She rolled on top of him, fitting their bodies together in all the right places. Then she kissed the corner of his eyes, his cheeks, his chin, his neck— definitely his neck—and that erotic zone right behind his ear. She nibbled every possible surface except his lips. She was saving those for last. He rubbed his hands up and down her back and then started kneading her buttocks. That was nice. Very, very nice.

Chad flipped her over and treated her to the same consideration. He wasn't content with exploring her face, though. He paid special attention to her breasts, licking and kissing them until she was moaning in anticipation. But even that wasn't enough. On the contrary, he went much, much lower…

Kelbie thought she might die from the sensation. What a way to go.

Chapter Thirty-Two

The past couple of days had been an emotional roller coaster. But now it was time for Chad to get back to business. He had a scheduled flight with Lt. Gavor this afternoon.

Lucky him!

It was a last-ditch effort to see if the guy had a chance of becoming a pilot. If he screwed this up he was out on his gold-plated rear end.

In the fall Wheatland was on the migratory path of birds escaping the frozen north. The runway supervisors tried their best to keep the feathered pests away, but they had a hard time doing so. And mixing birds with airplanes was like lighting a match near a natural gas leak. The chance of an explosion was pretty darn good.

Mere minutes after takeoff, Chad and Gavor encountered a flock of doves. And sure enough, the birds were quickly sucked into the engines. Both engines flamed out, the hydraulics failed and Chad's supersonic craft turned into a glider from hell. There was no way to steer it, no way to control it and no way to bring it down in one piece.

Damn it all!

Fear wafted off Gavor in waves. Chad had never punched out of an airplane, so he was none too calm himself. He hoped to God he sounded in control when he radioed the tower. This ordinary flight had turned into a high-stakes game of survival.

"Do *not* touch a thing," Chad instructed Gavor. He was trying to sound confident. The last thing he needed was for his terrified student to pull the ejection handle.

"Just sit there and don't move. I'll punch us out."

For now the momentum of the plane was keeping them in the air. Knowing that wouldn't last forever, Chad pulled the ejection handle as soon as they cleared the farmhouses below them. The canopy flew off and they were shot out by the rocket under their seats.

Jesus, Mary and Joseph! That was as much of a prayer as Chad could manage before his chute deployed. When he was jerked up, indicating he'd gotten a good parachute, he gave a huge sigh of relief. As Chad drifted toward the ground he could see Gavor a couple hundred yards away. He sure hoped the kid had paid attention to his parasailing instructor.

Off in the distance the plane hit the ground and erupted in a fireball. Fortunately, they were far enough away from the wreckage that the wind didn't blow them into the conflagration.

They were going to make it. And as amazing as it might seem, Gavor wasn't responsible for this disaster.

Shortly after they hit the ground, the rescue squad arrived, led by Dale Decker and Tim Fletcher. Chad had just freed himself from his parachute when his friend ran over to him. There were so many emergency personnel, both civilian and military, that the scene looked like a major disaster.

"Are you okay?" Dale had to yell to be heard over the chaos.

"I'm fine, but I don't know about him." Lt. Gavor was writhing on the ground, holding his ankle.

"Perhaps we should send him back to his home country to recuperate," Dale said with a smirk.

"I vote for that," Colonel Fletcher agreed. "But for now he's going to the hospital in town. I don't want to take any chances on his health. As for you—" he pointed at Chad "—you're going to the base clinic to get checked out."

When the boss man gave an order, the only acceptable response was "yes, sir." But before Chad hopped in the ambulance, he snagged Dale. "Make sure my kids and Kelbie know I'm not hurt."

TODAY WASN'T JUST ANY other day—it was the day after the best sexual experience she'd ever had. Kelbie was one well-loved babe. Erotic thoughts and prurient interests had transformed her into a blithering idiot.

Those delicious thoughts vanished when Sherry rushed in. "Harvey Hawkins just called and he said…he said—" She plopped in the chair, trying to catch her breath.

"Harvey Hawkins said what?" Kelbie spoke very slowly and deliberately. Harvey owned one of the largest farms in western Oklahoma.

"He called to tell us there's been a crash south of the base. He saw a plane go down."

No! This couldn't be happening—it simply wasn't possible. What were the odds of Chad being involved? Kelbie's brain told her she was being paranoid. But her heart galloped like a stampede of wild stallions.

She grabbed the phone. "I'll call Chad's cell and see what's going on." It rang and rang, but he didn't answer. That didn't mean a thing. He was probably in a meeting and didn't want to be disturbed. Although she was trying to put a positive spin on it, her sixth sense insisted that something terrible had happened, and she'd learned long ago not to ignore that bad boy.

"Let me try his office." Kelbie's hands were sweating so much she could barely hold the receiver. She was about to hang up when a sergeant finally answered.

"Hi, this is Kelbie Montgomery. May I speak to Colonel Cassavetes?" Her voice shook, but that was too darn bad.

"Ma'am, uh, let me transfer you to Lieutenant Colonel Decker. Hang on until someone over there picks up." He didn't wait for an answer before he disconnected.

Kelbie wasn't about to wade through all that bureaucratic crap. If Dale Decker had the information she needed, she'd go straight to the source—Amy Decker. Kelbie opened her computer phone book and frantically scrolled through the names. Bingo. And after a quick conversation with Amy, she had Dale's cell number.

"Decker here!"

"Dale, I hate to bother you, but do you know where Chad is?" She couldn't bear to ask the real question.

"Kelbie?"

"Yes, it's me."

"Don't freak out, but Chad was involved in a crash. He's fine, I promise. But I need you to do something for me. I was about to call Amy but you'll be better. Will you go pick up Hannah and Rachel at school?"

Oh God, oh God, oh God! Speech was impossible and cogent thought was making its way toward the exit.

"Well, uh, sure."

"The emergency technicians are taking Chad to the base clinic to be checked out. Just a minute." Dale's next words were muffled; his hand was obviously over the receiver. "I'm back. I'll call the school and make sure they don't give you a hard time about getting the kids. Take them to our house. I'm calling Amy right now. I gotta go. Everything's gonna be okay." Dale clicked off.

Kelbie stared at the receiver.

"Are you all right?" Sherry asked as she took the phone out of Kelbie's hand. "Why don't you sit down?"

She had totally forgotten that her friend was there. "Chad was in the crash and I need to go pick up the girls." She grabbed her purse and was halfway out the door as she added, "Take care of things around here. I'll call you when I can."

Dale said he was heading to the clinic. But was he badly hurt? No, Dale said he was okay and he wouldn't lie— would he? Chad was fine—that was Kelbie's single-minded mantra as she drove to the high school. She was the adult. She had to be strong.

Rachel went totally white when she discovered that Kelbie was taking her out of class in the middle of the day. "Why are you here? Is something wrong with Daddy? Is it Hannah?"

Kelbie put her arm around the teen. "I don't know any details, but Dale Decker asked me to get you and your sister and take you to his house. There's been an accident, but he told me your dad isn't hurt." That wasn't exactly what he'd said, but it was her story and she was sticking to it. At least until she was proved wrong—and she could only hope that wouldn't be the case.

ON THE DRIVE TO THE BASE, Hannah was crying, Rachel was silent as a stone and Kelbie was doing her best to be upbeat, not that she bought her own spiel.

Why hadn't Dale called her back? Where was Chad?

The symptoms of shock were all there: her heart was pounding, her palms were sweating and, swear to goodness, she was afraid she'd have to stop the truck and be sick.

Kelbie managed to get through the base gates with a minimum of hassle, and the minute she pulled into the drive, Amy came running out.

"Girls, good news!" she squealed before she pulled Hannah and Rachel into a motherly hug. "Your dad is fine. He's at the base clinic getting checked out and Dale will bring him home in a few minutes."

The pandemonium that ensued was both cathartic and joyous. But even through Kelbie's relief, her doubts started to nag her. Could she really live with the specter of losing him? Perhaps it was smarter to walk away now with at least part of her heart intact.

Kelbie knew the statistics concerning the safety of air force aviation. And yes, she realized there was a better chance of being struck by a bus than of dying in a crash. But today's accident had brought back memories and fears that she couldn't ignore.

Chapter Thirty-Three

Chad gingerly got out of Dale's SUV and Hannah and Rachel almost knocked him down. They wanted to hold his hand and hug his neck.

In contrast, Kelbie seemed withdrawn. That was understandable considering that the reunion had rapidly turned into a party. Perry AFB hadn't had a crash in a long time and people seemed to be letting out a collective sigh of relief. They realized a disaster had been averted, and were also grateful it hadn't happened to them. But Chad would've been just as happy to celebrate his survival quietly at home with his daughters and the woman he loved.

THE DECKERS' LIVING ROOM felt like New Year's Eve at Times Square. Kelbie wasn't sure she should even be there. She wasn't family, she wasn't part of the military community, and to be perfectly honest, she didn't know how to characterize her relationship with Chad.

Yesterday she'd thought they had something they could build on. Today it felt like a replay of the tragedy with Jason. Yes, Chad had survived the crash. Yes, it was an anomaly. And yes, he'd probably die in his sleep at ninety.

But what if it happened again? Could she dust herself off and start over one more time?

Kelbie felt the prickle of tears start at the back of her eyes. She knew that once she started crying she wouldn't be able to stop. She grabbed her coat and headed for the door, intent on escape. Then she caught sight of Chad across the room and knew she couldn't leave without talking to him.

"I need to speak to you for a second," she said when she reached his side.

"Sure." He put his hand under her elbow and led her toward the front of the house. "Let's go outside. It's getting hot in here."

Once they got to the carport Kelbie laid it all out—her fears, her hopes, everything. She felt compelled to touch him, so she wrapped her arms around his neck. She realized she was sending mixed signals, but it was the only way she could manage.

"When I heard that you were in an accident, I thought I was going to die."

"For a couple of seconds, I thought I was, too," Chad said with a chuckle.

"This isn't funny!" She was being a shrew but couldn't help herself.

"I know, sweetie. I know."

"I love you, but I need some time alone to think about our relationship." Just saying the words broke her heart.

"Kelbie, don't do this. Please, please don't do this."

She hated embarrassing exits but she couldn't stay there any longer. Kelbie rushed to her car, leaving Chad standing on the sidewalk.

Kelbie was pulling into her drive when her cell phone rang. Was she brave enough to answer? To put it simply, she couldn't decide whether she was ready to take a chance on love again.

She couldn't talk to Chad, at least not tonight. Hopefully, he'd take his kids home and leave her to stew in her indecision.

WHAT WAS GOING ON in that beautiful head of hers? Chad wondered. One day some lucky schmuck would decipher a woman's thought process and make a ton of money, but it wouldn't be today.

He told Amy what had happened and excused himself from the celebration. "Hop in the truck, kids. We're going out to the Montgomerys' house."

"Why?" Hannah asked.

"What's wrong? Is Mrs. Montgomery okay?" Rachel had obviously noticed Kelbie's disappearance.

"I don't know, but I intend to find out." Chad didn't break *all* the traffic rules, but he did bend a couple of them.

Kelbie's truck was in front of her house. It looked as if it had been parked by a New York cabbie. "Why don't you guys go to the barn and check on the horses. I'll be down in a minute."

"Are you sure?" Rachel asked.

"Everything's gonna be fine." Chad resisted the urge to add "I promise."

He waited until the kids walked across the paddock before he rang the doorbell.

When Kelbie opened the door, Chad noticed that she'd already changed into jeans and a sweatshirt. Her greeting was less than effusive. "I wish you hadn't followed me. I really need to be alone right now."

The situation wasn't looking good.

"This all has to do with your husband's crash, doesn't

it?" If he said anything else on the subject she'd probably hit him, so Chad kept his mouth shut.

"Yes, it does."

"Couldn't we sit down and talk this out? We can make this work, I know we can. Please." He wasn't above begging.

"I can't. Not tonight."

Chad didn't lose his temper often, but this time he figured it was justified. "In case you hadn't noticed, I was in a plane crash today. Don't you care that I could've been killed?" That was the worst thing he could possibly have said. It was exactly what they were arguing about.

Kelbie's every thought was visible on her face. She realized that what they had was special, but she wasn't willing to fight for it. The pink on her cheeks deepened to crimson. "I think we should cool this, uh, whatever it is we have going."

"You think we should cool this *whatever?*" Chad's tone was dripping with sarcasm. Damn his luck with women. "Okay. In the future I'll get Stacy to drive the girls to the barn. Sorry to bother you." He turned on his heel and stomped across the pasture.

Chapter Thirty-Four

The past week had been absolutely miserable. Why did doing the right thing feel so wrong? The answer was easy—she was madly in love with Chad and had royally mucked things up. "Does that make you feel any better?" Marge asked as she spooned up a dollop of whipped cream.

Kelbie's drug of choice was a supersize banana split. It helped only if she didn't dwell on the erotic nature of her last banana split. "Yes!" she snapped. Since breaking up with Chad, she was alternately depressed and snippy. Sometimes she was downright rude. In other words, she was making everyone around her crazy.

Marge gave her the narrow-eyed glare she usually reserved for naughty kids and out-of-control inmates. "You know what the problem is, don't you?"

Kelbie couldn't help but glare right back at her friend. Of course she knew what the problem was.

"So what are you going to do about it?" Marge asked.

She wasn't being a busybody. She was simply trying to help—as had several other well-meaning folks. For the moment, though, all Kelbie wanted to do was wallow in her own misery, and how melodramatic was that? What she needed was someone to slap some sense into her. The problem was no one seemed to be that brave.

Apparently Marge had volunteered. "You know that when Sam goes off to school you're going to be a lonely, lonely woman, don't you? And years later you'll be a bitter old hag with dozens of cats." Leave it to her friend to go straight to the heart of the matter.

"So what? I can do without men. Until the vaunted Colonel Cassavetes came on the scene I hadn't had a date in so long I was like a spinster in one of those old gothic novels. It didn't kill me then and it won't kill me now."

Marge snorted. "You're a piece of work, ya know that?" She didn't bother to wait for an answer. "Let me put it in terms that might get through that thick skull of yours." She leaned back and shot Kelbie the look again. "If there was a bus wreck out on I-20, say it skidded off the highway and went in the river, would you keep Sam from riding on a school bus again? Or to make it even more ridiculous, would you tell her she couldn't go swimming again?"

"That's dumb."

"Perhaps. But here's another one. What if there was a shooting on a campus in California. Would you tell your daughter she can't go to college because it might not be safe, or that she can't ever go to San Francisco?"

Although her friend had a way of cutting through the clutter, Kelbie wasn't ready to surrender. She was carrying around enough self-pity to last a couple of decades.

Good old Marge wasn't finished yet. "And on the more practical side, what's wrong with an adventure? Is it absolutely necessary for you to molder in this town?"

Her friend knew that one of Kelbie's reservations about Chad had been the military moves. "Who knows, you might go to Florida," she continued. "Or North Dakota. Or you might not have to go anywhere at all, at least not until Sam's in college."

There *was* something enticing about the idea of an adventure, not that Kelbie was willing to admit that to anyone.

She took a bite of chocolate courage. "Do you think I can fix this? He was really angry when he left. And I haven't heard anything from him in a week. Hannah tells me he's being a real bear."

Marge grinned. "It's a good sign that he's cranky. That means he still cares. When love's involved almost nothing is unattainable."

Almost? Was Marge hinting that this might be an impossible mission?

"I'm not saying I'm going to do this, but what's your idea?"

"I suggest that we get his kids involved." A woman would have to be desperate to resort to such an underhanded strategy, but Kelbie knew she was responsible for this debacle. And she also realized that if she didn't grab happiness with both hands she'd end up just like Marge predicted—a bitter old spinster. So maybe…

Luck was on her side. Rachel was alone in the barn, grooming Ariel.

"Would you mind if we talked about your dad?" Kelbie hoped the kid wouldn't take a pitchfork to her.

Rachel patted her horse's neck and stepped back. "If you have an idea, I'm all ears. Dad is acting looney. He just mopes around. Hannah and I are ready for an intervention." She grinned. "I saw that on TV."

"What would you think if your dad and I could get together?" Kelbie figured she'd tackle the hard question first. "If we got married, you and Sam would be stepsisters. Would you mind?"

Rachel shrugged. "I think that would be okay, and so does Hannah. We've talked about it." The teen grabbed Kelbie's hand. It was her first overt show of affection, and it touched Kelbie's heart.

"If you're worried about moving, Hannah and I haven't done it a lot but coming here wasn't bad."

Wasn't that sweet? The child was trying to reassure the adult.

"So, do you want to help me?"

"Right on!"

"What do you think we should do?" Kelbie wanted to get her perspective on the situation.

Rachel pursed her lips. "We need a reason for you guys to see each other, right?"

"Right."

"And what do you have in common?"

Kelbie didn't have to think twice. "You girls."

Rachel grinned. "Exactly."

"What kind of plan are you cooking up?"

"Remember when Hannah got hurt at that show?"

Kelbie couldn't believe she was even listening to this, much less contemplating being a coconspirator. "Yeah?"

"I'm a really good actress—you can ask Hannah. Lindsay Lohan should be shaking in her stilettos," Rachel said with a smirk. "Here's that we'll do."

LATER THAT AFTERNOON, Chad's admin assistant stuck his head in the office door. "That Marge lady from the barn is on the phone. She wants to talk to you."

Lately everything was a catastrophe. He picked up the receiver.

"Hi, Marge. What's up?"

"Rachel's horse went a little loco and she's pretty hysterical. Can you come out and help calm her down?"

"Is Rachel okay other than being upset?"

"I think so. I'll tell her you'll be here in about fifteen minutes." She didn't bother to let him answer before she hung up.

"I have an emergency. I have to go," he told his assistant, who was still lingering in the doorway. "Call me on my cell if you really need me."

Chad made it across town in record time. He raced his truck down the gravel drive, parked next to Kelbie's truck and ran into the barn.

"Daddy!" Hannah squealed as she jumped into his arms. "Rachel's crying."

"I know, honey. Let me put you down and I'll go see what's happening."

Rachel was sitting in the bleachers talking to Sam, but the moment she spotted Chad she started wailing. Huh. That was definitely fishy.

Sam took off as Chad sat down beside to his daughter. "Can you tell me in a hundred words or less what happened?"

Rachel sniffed. "I had Ariel tied to her stall door. There was a noise and when she pulled back, she got her foot caught in a bucket and went nutso. She bucked and bucked." She gave him a cow-eyed look that he hadn't seen before. "I was really scared." It was classic overacting. Rachel might be a drama queen but he was pretty sure Hollywood wasn't in her future.

Kelbie strolled over and put her arm around Rachel. "The horse is fine and the kid's okay. I'm sorry we called you."

Chad caught the look Rachel shot Kelbie. There was something very suspicious going on; he just didn't know who was involved.

"Kelbie, may I speak to you privately?"

"Sure. Rachel, why don't you go check on Ariel? Sam and Hannah are grooming her."

Chad waited until Rachel was out of earshot before he asked the burning question. "What's really going on?" He could smell a conspiracy in the air.

Kelbie covered her face with her hands and sighed before looking up at him. "Nothing happened with Ariel. This was a plot to get you out here," she confessed. "Now I'm feeling guilty. We shouldn't have scared you."

That was interesting—very, very interesting.

"You could've just called me yourself. You know I would've come. I was the one who wanted us to talk about our problems, remember?"

"I know. This was all my fault. And I was the one who approached Rachel, so don't get mad at her. At the time I thought it was a good idea."

"So you wanted to see me, but didn't know if I'd come?"

"Yeah."

"Would you like to go for coffee?"

"Sure. How about the Dairy Queen?" she asked with a grin.

"Perfect." That place had a lot of good memories.

THIS TIME, THEY SKIPPED the chocolate temptation and went straight for the more practical cup of coffee. Having a conversation with Chad was exactly what Kelbie had been hoping for. If he was really through with her, and he simply wanted to let her down gently, she'd muddle through somehow. But she certainly hoped that wouldn't be the case.

"I'm really sorry we tricked you."

"If these incidents weren't giving me gray hair I'd think this was funny." Chad ran his fingers through his completely not gray hair in the gesture she'd always thought endearing.

Kelbie foind it amazing that in the short time she'd known Chad he'd become such an integral part of her life. Grief, separation, happiness and love were all a part of living. She accepted that now. She couldn't take the good without the bad. The only constant was change, and life with Chad was worth the risk.

"I've missed you," she admitted.

His head snapped up. She'd scored a direct hit.

"Honestly?"

"No kidding." It was one of those now-or-never moments. What he said next would affect the rest of their lives.

"I've missed you, too." Chad took her hand. "Whatever our problems are, we can solve them if we work together. Do you love me?"

Leave it to a man to ask the right question. *"Yes."*

"Then there isn't anything we can't figure out, is there?"

He turned her hand over and kissed the base of each finger.

When he put it that way, who was she to argue? "I suppose there isn't. The older girls are even getting along most of the time." Kelbie laughed. "I have a feeling we'll have our hands full with those two. So, where exactly do you see this going?"

"We're getting married."

She arched an eyebrow, determined to make him work for this one. "Oh, really?"

Then Chad surprised the heck out of her. He scooted out of the booth and dropped down on one knee. "Kelbie Mont-gomery, I love you with all my heart and it would mean the world to me if you'd agree to be my wife."

If Kelbie accepted his proposal she had to be open to making concessions. "I'm willing to move. Marge said she'll buy the barn."

"I'll get out of the air force." Their statements were almost simultaneous. It was straight out of "The Gift of the Magi."

Life with Chad would be so entertaining. All the problems she'd chewed on in the dark of night *could* be solved. It didn't matter if they stayed here or if they moved; as long as they were a family everything would be fine.

"Well…" Kelbie pretended to mull it over, but the minute he pulled a plastic Cracker Jack ring out of his flight suit she broke into giggles. "Yes, you ninny. Of course I'll marry you."

"In case you're wondering why I had this, Hannah gave it to me. The kid obviously knew more than we did."

Chapter Thirty-Five

The Wheatland Review
November 15, 2009
Lieutenant Colonel Chad Cassavetes and Kelbie Harrison Montgomery were married in a small ceremony at the Wheatland First Methodist Church. The bride's attendants, Rachel Cassavetes, Samantha Montgomery and Hannah Cassavetes, wore matching denim skirts, ruffled Western blouses and pink cowboy boots. The reception, held in the indoor arena at Prairie View Farm, was catered by Pearlie May's Diner.

It was after midnight before Chad could convince his bride it was time to leave the reception. They had things to do— wink, wink. But even more exciting was the news he'd received early that morning.

They made their getaway in a hail of birdseed. Chad couldn't wait until they got to their hotel room. Once they made it to Oklahoma City they'd have more important things on their minds. So he pulled into the first parking lot he saw.

"Don't tell me we're staying here." Kelbie giggled.

Uh-oh. The gaudy red-and-green neon sign flashed its Sleep Here Motel message. In his haste, Chad had picked the worst place in town to stop.

"I promise we'll only be a second. I have something I can't wait to tell you."

"What?"

"I talked to Dave Carpenter. He's the directing manager of the Gen Tech Corporation, the folks who have the contract to run the base. He offered me a job as his codirector."

"Do you mean you'd retire from the air force to stay in Wheatland?" Kelbie couldn't believe what she was hearing. "What did you tell him?"

"That I had a wedding to go to and I'd come by and talk to him when I got back."

Kelbie didn't know what they'd eventually decide, but she did know that together, they'd make the right decision.

And it really didn't matter where they lived as long as they had each other.

* * * * *

*Celebrate 60 years of pure reading pleasure
with Harlequin®!*

To commemorate the event, Silhouette Special
Edition invites you to Ashley O'Ballivan's bed-and-
breakfast in the small town of Stone Creek. The beautiful innkeeper will have her hands full caring for her
old flame Jack McCall. He's on the run and recov-
ering from a mysterious illness, but that won't stop
him from trying to win Ashley back.

*Enjoy an exclusive glimpse of Linda Lael Miller's
AT HOME IN STONE CREEK
Available in November 2009
from Silhouette Special Edition®.*

The helicopter swung abruptly sideways in a dizzying arch, setting Jack McCall's fever-ravaged brain spinning.

His friend's voice sounded tinny, coming through the earphones. "You belong in a hospital," he said. "Not some backwater bed-and-breakfast."

All Jack really knew about the virus raging through his system was that it wasn't contagious, and there was no known treatment for it besides a lot of rest and quiet. "I don't like hospitals," he responded, hoping he sounded like his normal self. "They're full of sick people."

Vince Griffin chuckled but it was a dry sound, rough at the edges. "What's in Stone Creek, Arizona?" he asked. "Besides a whole lot of nothin'?"

Ashley O'Ballivan was in Stone Creek, and she was a whole lot of somethin', but Jack had neither the strength nor the inclination to explain. After the way he'd ducked out six months before, he didn't expect a welcome, knew he didn't deserve one. But Ashley, being Ashley, would take him in whatever her misgivings.

He had to get to Ashley; he'd be all right.

He closed his eyes, letting the fever swallow him.

There was no telling how much time had passed when he

became aware of the chopper blades slowing overhead. Dimly, he saw the private ambulance waiting on the airfield outside of Stone Creek; it seemed that twilight had descended.

Jack sighed with relief. His clothes felt clammy against his flesh. His teeth began to chatter as two figures unloaded a gurney from the back of the ambulance and waited for the blades to stop.

"Great," Vince remarked, unsnapping his seat belt. "Those two look like volunteers, not real EMTs."

The chopper bounced sickeningly on its runners, and Vince, with a shake of his head, pushed open his door and jumped to the ground, head down.

Jack waited, wondering if he'd be able to stand on his own. After fumbling unsuccessfully with the buckle on his seat belt, he decided not.

When it was safe the EMTs approached, following Vince, who opened Jack's door.

His old friend Tanner Quinn stepped around Vince, his grin not quite reaching his eyes.

"You look like hell warmed over," he told Jack cheerfully.

"Since when are you an EMT?" Jack retorted.

Tanner reached in, wedged a shoulder under Jack's right arm and hauled him out of the chopper. His knees immediately buckled, and Vince stepped up, supporting him on the other side.

"In a place like Stone Creek," Tanner replied, "everybody helps out."

They reached the wheeled gurney, and Jack found himself on his back.

Tanner and the second man strapped him down, a process that brought back a few bad memories.

"Is there even a hospital in this place?" Vince asked irritably from somewhere in the night.

"There's a pretty good clinic over in Indian Rock," Tanner answered easily, "and it isn't far to Flagstaff." He paused to help his buddy hoist Jack and the gurney into the back of the ambulance. "You're in good hands, Jack. My wife is the best veterinarian in the state."

Jack laughed raggedly at that.

Vince muttered a curse.

Tanner climbed into the back beside him, perched on some kind of fold-down seat. The other man shut the doors.

"You in any pain?" Tanner said as his partner climbed into the driver's seat and started the engine.

"No." Jack looked up at his oldest and closest friend and wished he'd listened to Vince. Ever since he'd come down with the virus—a week after snatching a five-year-old girl back from her non-custodial parent, a small-time Colombian drug dealer—he hadn't been able to think about anyone or anything but Ashley. When he *could* think, anyway.

Now, in one of the first clearheaded moments he'd experienced since checking himself out of Bethesda the day before, he realized he might be making a major mistake. Not by facing Ashley—he owed her that much and a lot more. No, he could be putting her in danger, putting Tanner and his daughter and his pregnant wife in danger, too.

"I shouldn't have come here," he said, keeping his voice low.

Tanner shook his head, his jaw clamped down hard as though he was irritated by Jack's statement.

"This is where you belong," Tanner insisted. "If you'd had sense enough to know that six months ago, old buddy, when you bailed on Ashley without so much as a fare-thee-well, you wouldn't be in this mess."

Ashley. The name had run through his mind a million times in those six months, but hearing somebody say it out loud was like having a fist close around his insides and squeeze hard.

Jack couldn't speak.

Tanner didn't press for further conversation.

The ambulance bumped over country roads, finally hitting smooth blacktop.

"Here we are," Tanner said. "Ashley's place."

* * * * *

*Will Jack be able to
patch things up with Ashley, or will his past put the
woman he loves in harm's way?
Find out in
AT HOME IN STONE CREEK
by Linda Lael Miller
Available November 2009
from Silhouette Special Edition®.*